Girls Like Us

Girls Like Us

GAIL GILES

CANDLEWICK PRESS

First edition 2014

Library of Congress Catalog Card Number 2013944011
ISBN 978-0-7636-6267-7

14 15 16 17 18 19 BVG 10 9 8 7 6 5 4 3 2 1

Printed in Berryville, VA, U.S.A.

This book was typeset in Adobe Garamond Pro.

Candlewick Press
99 Dover Street
Somerville, Massachusetts 02144

visit us at www.candlewick.com

*Always and always and always
for Jim Giles and Josh Jakubik,
my heroes*

Biddy

My name is Biddy.

Some call me other names.

Granny call me Retard.

Quincy call me White Trash sometimes and Fool most of the time.

Most kids call me Speddie. That's short for Special Education.

I can't write or read. A little bit, but not good enough to matter.

There's a lots of stuff I don't know. If I could write, I could make a long list. List might reach all the way through Texas to someplace like Chicago. I don't know where Chicago is. That's another thing for the list.

But there's some things I do know. And once I know a thing, I hold it tight and don't let it stray off.

Granny shouldn't call me Retard. I know that. It ain't nice. It hurts my feelings.

I know it's a wrong thing to hurt somebody's feelings. I know that I ain't White Trash. Trash is something you throw away. You don't throw nobody away. That's wrong. Even if my mama done it to me.

Quincy

Most folk call me Quincy. I ain't pretty but I got me a pretty name. My whole name be Sequencia.

The one thing all us Speddies can tell you is what kind of retard we are. Ms. Evans get wadded in a knot if anybody say retarded. We be "differently abled." We be "mentally challenged," she say. I got challenged when my mama's boyfriend hit my head with a brick.

I was six and I remember being smarter. My mama and her boyfriend was fighting, and I turnt the TV up so I could hear my show. The door was helt open to let air in with an ole brick that had cement stuck on it. Mama's boyfriend pick up that brick and hit me. Kinda over my eye and the side of my head.

They's still a big ole dent in my head, and one of my eyes is push down. My face look like somebody put both hands on it and push up on one side and pull down on the other.

I got took away from my mama, and the doctor say that I got brain damage from that brick. I don't know. My mama was a crack ho, so I wasn't gonna be too smart no how.

People think when you in Special Ed that you s'posed to be sitting 'round drooling so they can pick you right out the crowd. That just shows they be dumber than they think we are. There's folks in Special Ed get driver's licenses. They go to school, hand you change at the store, take your order at the drive-through, and sack your groceries. We talk just like other folk. We— well, not me, but most—look just like other folk. We understand stuff. We just learn it slow. And most of what we understand is that people what ain't Speddies think we too stupid to get out our own way. And that makes me mad.

Biddy

I don't know my mama's name. Granny says she don't want to hear that no-count name in her ears, much less let it walk on her tongue. All she'll say is that my mama showed up one day, dirty and stinking and toting me. She told Granny she wanted to spend the night. When Granny woke up the next morning, Mama flown the coop. And I was roosting.

She said she knew something was wrong when I was a year old. I hadn't turned over by myself. A visiting nurse took me to a hospital. Doctor said I had moderate retardation. Two big words, but I know them. I thought they was my last name. "This is Biddy," Granny would say. "She's moderate retardation."

The doctor said that not enough oxygen got to my brain when I was being borned. And that's why I'm slow. And that means I couldn't give it to my baby. That's why Granny could give her away. If she been a stupid child, I maybe could have kept her.

I guess I love Granny. She took me in and fed me. She tells me about it all the time. But she calls me mean names. Maybe I know why my mama left Granny's place. What I can't get hold of is why, knowing what she did, my mama didn't take me with her.

Graduation is coming up. Part of me is glad. I won't have to get on the school bus no more. I won't have to walk past boys that laugh that dirty laugh. Throw candy wrappers at me. But I been scaredy feeling. Granny said I can't live with her after graduation. She said the state don't send no more checks now. I'm past eighteen and graduating. Said I been roosting too long in her nest.

Where would I be if I wasn't at Granny's? I don't know how to be nowhere else. My stomach hurt for a whole bunch of days worrying about it.

Quincy

Well, if I ain't lower than a snake's butt. I was feeling fine 'bout graduation coming up. Thinking to myself, Won't that show my ole mama? Here I am, with a dented head and still manage to graduate. Then Ms. Evans call me and that fool Biddy in her office.

"I've got terrific news for you," Ms. Evans say, all smiling and proud.

Then she slap me upside the head with news almost hard as that brick. She tole me that since I'm eighteen and graduating, I cain't stay with my foster fambly no more. Then she say that everything was fine. Since me and another girl was wards of the state, we would be took care of. I was going to live with the other girl and have a job. I had me a bad feeling then. Why ole fat Biddy in the office too?

"You and Biddy are going to be roommates," Ms. Evans say, like she'd just hand me chocolate cake with a money filling.

I look over at Biddy and she smiling so big I can practally see the inside her toes, but I cain't believe what I'm hearin'.

Biddy in my Living Skills class. That stupid cow cain't read or write. I can. I'm in Special Education like her, but I take regular reading and math classes.

One day in Living Skills, I tole Ms. Evans that in my reading class we had to keep us a journal. Write in it every day. I have myself a hard time writing, and it tire me out sumpin' awful. Ms. Evans say she can fix me right up. She go to the closet and brung out this little tape recorder and a pile of tapes.

"Ask your teacher if it's OK if you use this. Instead of writing, you can keep an oral journal."

I give her a "What that mean?" look.

She smile. I love the way that woman smile. She got the whitest, straightest teeth, and they shine out her dark face.

"'Oral' means spoken. You might tell your story out loud instead of writing it down."

Biddy, she got ears 'bout big as her buffalo butt.

"What's a journal?"

Ms. Evans turnt around and talk to that ole tub and forget clean about me. "A journal is like a diary. You write, or tell, your thoughts every day. It's a story about yourself."

I swear, Biddy don't know how to hide a thing. Everything she think just hop up and sit on that ashy white face for anybody to see. Her face brighten up like somebody turnt on a lamp in front of a mirror. "Could I do that? Tell my story to the tape?"

And there she go. Elbow her way into sumpin' of mine. Now she doin' it again with this livin' together thing.

Then Ms. Evans tell Biddy she gonna take her to buy a dress for graduation. For a present. Biddy's face look like — I don't know — a full moon rising over a corn patch.

I don't need me no charity dresses. I got me a new pink lacy one.

But Biddy. Woo, that girl need some dressing. Seem like in middle school she dress poor, but not . . . well, not like she do now. She start that ugly thing after what happen in seventh grade. Since then, shoot-a-goose, that girl a pure mess. She got this pair of navy-blue stretch pants done stretch way too far. I swear she wear 'em every day. She got three T-shirts, huge ones, maybe cover up a king-size bed. I got to say, the girl don't stink, so she must wash those things right often.

But the big deal is that coat. It's a long tan coat, and Biddy wear it all the time. All the time. We live in Texas, right on the Gulf, and it's hot, but Biddy wearing that coat summer and winter, in class and out. I never seen that girl without her coat.

One day, I found out why. Rosie DeVries is a mean

ole stick that make fun of folk. She trailer trash and not much count herself, but she think 'cause she white and not a Speddie that she somebody important. Anyway, she find out a few months ago that she can make Biddy go crazy if she tease her long enough. One day, Rosie must have been in a real bad mood, 'cause she start in hard on ole Rhino Hino. Call her names—well, Rhino Hino one of them—I didn't think that up my ownself. And she axt Biddy if she had any other pants and did her Granny feed her slops to get so fat. Biddy start to wailing and crying. Lord, snot and tears running like a garden hose.

Then Biddy got mad enough to say something back. "You leave me alone, you bitch!"

Nobody ever heard Biddy say a cuss word. Everybody watching drop they mouth open, until we looked like a bunch of gasper-goos flung up on the bank.

That light a flame under Rosie. She reach out and grab Biddy's arm and yank hard. It swing Biddy around and pop the buttons on that raggedy tan coat and it fly open.

Pin to the inside of her coat was candy bars, bags of chips, packages of peanut-butter crackers, little sacks of cookies, and all kinds of stuff. The girl a vending machine with feets.

Rosie laugh so hard that she forget she was mad.

"This ho's got a sto' in her coat." She laugh again. "The ho with the sto." Most everybody laugh. Biddy pull her coat up over her face and run off to the bathroom.

I didn't laugh. I know what it's like for folk to call you names.

But I didn't help neither. Besides, everybody know Biddy be a ho.

Biddy

Graduation was good. I wore my new dress. I combed my hair real nice. I didn't mind looking nice at my graduation, in the light. With all those peoples watching. With Ms. Evans there—I didn't think nothing bad could happen.

Ms. Evans said that me and Quincy are the only Speddies graduating this year. I feel extra special about graduating. Like I done something good. We got in an adult program. We'll live in a little house. Maybe we will even end up being friends together. And a counselor will check us. That makes me feel all safe and good. We even got jobs! I'm gonna clean house and do for an old lady. Our house is on top of her garage. It's the best thing that ever happened to me.

Another teacher, the one across the hall from our Living Skills room, give me a watch. We lined up to walk on the football field. Ms. Evans come and handed me a rose.

I hadn't even seen that all the other girls got roses to carry. Maybe they parents give 'em to 'em. That was real nice of Ms. Evans. But it made me lonely. I don't know why.

We marched on the field, and peoples in the stands clapped. It made me smile. When my name was called, I marched right up to the stand. I got my diploma. I was so excited. I shook everybody hand. I started back down. I got a little confused. Ms. Evans came and got me back to my seat. It was OK again.

Granny didn't come. She said my paper ain't nothin' but a joke. She says that I didn't have no real classes. It ain't a real diploma.

Quincy

Lordy, graduation was sumpin'. I had me a fine pink dress and a rose, and I walked myself proud and straight-backed onto that football field. Took my diploma and shake the principal's hand like we been showed, then walk back to my seat. That durned tassel thing tickle my nose, but I didn't scratch it or nothing.

Biddy, I swear that girl. She smile so big, you could put her diploma in her mouth crostways. She practally run up that platform and snatch her certificate from the principal's hand. She grab his hand and pump it like she be getting water, then she shaking hands with the other folks on the platform. Just a-babbling at 'em. She shake every single person's hand—even the cop guard! Then she start back to her seat, but she turnt wrong and start loping right off the field. Ms. Evans had to get her turnt around.

And I got to live with this fool. I must've done something bad awful that I got to bear this cross. Leastwise, if I live with her, I finally be the smartest person in the house.

Biddy

Quincy and me met up at the high school with Ms. Evans and our new counselor, Ms. Delamino. I like to say her name real slow. With my nose a little bit up in the air like smart people on the TV.

Ms. Delamino rode us in her car to meet the lady that I'm going to do for. Her last name is longer than Ms. Delamino's. It's hard to get hold of, so I'm gonna call her Miss Lizzy. Ms. Delamino say Miss Lizzy was married to the mayor. But he done died a few years back. She had her a sometime housekeeper. Now she need all-the-time help.

When we got there, I couldn't believe my own eyes. Miss Lizzy live in a house that look like it come straight out a storybook. Great big front porch that you got to walk up a couple of steps to get to. A door with glass in a big egg shape. Ms. Delamino tapped on the door and opened it. She called out Miss Lizzy last name. Said that we was here. I stood in the hall and look up. I never knew a ceiling in a house could be so tall up in the air. And a light with hanging-down pieces of glass that twinkled and shined was over my head. Under my feet was wood floor with a long, skinny rug covering a lots of it. That rug was thick enough to sleep on.

"Please come in." That's when I saw Miss Lizzy. She was in a room off to the side of the hall. Ms. Delamino walked into that fancy room. Shook Miss Lizzy's hand. She waved at Quincy and me to come in. She told Miss Lizzy our names.

Miss Lizzy's real little. With silver hair. Eyes so black they look shiny. She wore a dress-up suit and stood in a walker thing. She looked me over real hard and said, "Honey, you look like an angel come down to earth. Don't know why you're wearing that coat in the summer, though."

I stared at my shoes. I couldn't think if I ought to say thank you or I'm sorry.

Miss Lizzy pushed her walker to Quincy. She put her hand up to Quincy's bad cheek and said, "You poor dear. Nobody will hurt you here."

Quincy jerked away and sulled up. Sometimes I don't know about that girl.

We went with Ms. Delamino to see our house. We climb the white stairs nextside of the garage. I felt like the princess going up to the castle. We went in. It was the prettiest place I ever did see. The kitchen look like it come from a dollhouse. So cute and tidy. There's a counter that has stools at it, so we don't need a table. The furniture isn't broke down and the walls are clean.

No peeling wallpaper or brown water stains nowhere. And two bedrooms! I never had me a bedroom before. Granny stored stacks of old newspaper and magazines and all her mail in the extra bedroom in her house. I slept on a pallet in the living room.

Quincy picked her room first. Mine is painted white and has a bed made of curly metal. It's painted white too. It has a pretty quilt on it. It has a table nextside of the bed with a fancy cloth on it that reaches all the way to the floor. It's got yellow and blue flowers. I never saw anything so nice. I turned myself in a circle. I put my arms out wide, just to feel the pretty. I'll work hard all the day to live in a place so nice and clean.

Quincy

Our apartment/house 'bout as big as a hummingbird's nest but it ain't so bad. It only gots a shower and I like me a good soaking tub, but I can get along pretty good here, long as that stick of an ole woman be leavin' me alone. Ms. D. tell us she take us to our houses to collect our things. Biddy run outside, then come back in with a paper sack. Everything that girl own in a little ole sack. I shake my head.

Biddy scoot into her room and thump her pitiful sack on her bed. She start whirling 'round like she Cinderella and babbling 'bout her "princess table." Under the raggedy flower sheet, her "table" just a turnt-over garbage can. Girl can't see past the stars in her eyes. "I'm moved in. I'm home to stay," she say, smiling so big her cheeks 'bout hide her eyes.

If I had eyes that wasn't mashed up by a brick, I sure 'nuff wouldn't hide 'em behind a bunch a fat. I guess when even ole witch ladies call her purty and say she look like a angel, Biddy got something to smile about, fat or not. It ain't like she earn being purty.

Ms. D. tole Biddy to put her stuff away and get comfortable while she take me to get my clothes. Most foster childs learn to live pretty light; I had me three boxes and a suitcase, anyways. I tole my foster mama good-bye, promised I'd let her know how I was doing. She invite me to have Thanksgiving with them and such like that. She try to give me a hug and a kiss. Shoot-a-goose! I pull away fast-like. These last foster parents was good enough people, but I never felt no mush to any of my foster famblies. Ain't any use in that. Get move too often.

We get back to the garage-house, and the floor was mop and wax to a shine that made my eyes water. Biddy had all the stuff pull out the bottom cabinets and was washing the insides. Her whole head was in them cabinets, and her big butt just a-waggling out there in the breeze whilst she scrub. Fool singing 'bout the Itsy-Bitsy Spider.

I don't laugh much. Don't see much that's funny. But I sat myself down on that saggy couch and bust a gut.

Biddy

I don't know about that Quincy. Here we moved to the prettiest place. It's all our own. Miss Lizzy is sweet as can be. She treated us like we was somebody real important, but Quincy stayed puffed up. Then she come back with her things. Plop down on the couch. And she's cackling like a hen on a nest.

I laugh too. Just be friendly.

Ms. Delamino sat us down. Told us we had to get to business. She told me what I was to do for Miss Lizzy. Clean that big pretty house. Help Miss Lizzy do her exercises. Cook her meals. I look down at my shoes on that one. Ms. Delamino said, "What's wrong, Biddy? Can't you cook?"

"'Course she can cook. Anybody can cook," Quincy say.

I nod my head fast. I know Quincy's smart. If she says anybody can cook, maybe it's that way.

Ms. Delamino told Quincy she got her a job in the bakery part of the Brown Cow grocery store. She started in to talking about paying bills and handling money. My mind got tired.

"Can we get us a TV?"

Ms. Delamino looked at me. Quincy flapped her hand. "Hush, we talking bidness here. Go clean a cabinet or something."

That sound OK to me.

Quincy

"Can we get us a TV?" that ole fool say.

Here we be, starting our real lives, and she off wool-gathering about Satiddy morning cartoons. What I'm going do with this girl? She white, she fat, she stupid, and she a ho. I gotta say, though, that girl clean like nobody's bidness. I like a clean place, but I cain't say I like sweeping and mopping. I knew when I see Biddy look down at her toes, like she waiting for 'em to do tricks, that I be free of scrubbing. After Ms. D. leave, me and Biddy gonna do like I hear in the movies. Gonna have us a power lunch and do us a deal.

Ms. D. and I talk bidness, and some of it I forget 'bout as soon as she say it, but she write it all down for me to study on. We get to live here, and the electricity, phone, and suchlike paid for as part of Biddy's earnings. All we got to buy is food and clothes. And long-distance calls—like we got friends to call far away. Or close-by ones.

Ms. D. gimme a chart that show what each of us be paying for. She said to divide up the housekeeping chores our ownselfs. We can do our laundry in the ole lady's house and eat the vegetables from the side-yard garden. My ears perk right up at that. I love fresh vegetables. Ms. D. say she gonna come check on us, and twice a month she'll help us get our 'spenses straight.

I was sure enough ready to get her out my face when Ms. D. up and leave. She gonna take me to my job tomorrow morning. She axt do we have a 'larm clock. Biddy say the rooster at her house always wake her up.

Ms. D. didn't much know what to say to that. I shore did.

"Fool, you bring that rooster in your raggedy little sack?"

I 'spect Biddy to get all mad or teared up, but she get her face in a puzzle-knot. "No, Granny wouldn't let me take nothing but my clothes."

I had to half feel sorry for the girl then.

"I got a 'larm clock," I say to Ms. D.

She nod and say she gonna leave us to it. I was glad enough to get shed of her. She lean down and whisper in my ear. "Try to get along. Enough people have been mean to Biddy. She doesn't need you to start. And it's as important to you as it is to her that this project work out."

I felt a little shamed, like I'd step on a new-laid egg. But the next thing I know, I hear Biddy singing "Itsy-Bitsy Spider," and I look 'round to see that big ole butt waggling out the cabinet again.

Biddy

Quincy said, "Let's us go down and see that garden."

I wanted to finish up scrubbing. But I wanted to be nice to Quincy too. So I follow her downstairs.

It sure was a pretty garden. Vegetables growing in nice straight rows. Things that are tidy and straight make me feel good. That's why I know how to clean. And I had lots of practice scrubbing up after Granny.

There was scrawny green things growing in a by-itself place.

"I can clear those weeds," I told Quincy.

"Them ain't no weeds; them is herbs."

"What that?" I ask her.

Quincy rolled her eyes. "Make food taste good. Don't you fret 'bout that. Just don't go pulling 'em up when you gets a cleaning fit."

She told me to pick three big tomatoes. She went to plucking some of the herb-weeds. She pulled something she called spring onions and a skinny lettuce plant.

I know what vegetables are. But Granny didn't never buy any. I guess we was about to eat a few now. I'm starting my brand-new life.

Quincy

That garden nice as the one Mr. Hallis had. He was one of my foster daddies. Biddy and me got some stuff together and went on upstairs. This was the first part of my plan not be doing no housework.

I pull out a can of chicken. I'd rather use fresh, but this be fine for today. I wash the tomatoes and cut 'em open. I mix the chicken up with a little mayo and my secret weapon—blue cheese dressing. Then I mince some basil up 'long with those green onions. I spoon the chicken into the tomatoes and sprinkle the basil and onion on the top. I put a couple sprigs of parsley into the chicken to purty it up.

Biddy look at those plates. "I never did eat nothing like that."

That ain't a surprise. All I ever see Biddy eat at school was potato chips and candy bars. She didn't get to be no Buffalo Butt from snackin' on lettuce and carrots.

"Well, this here is Quincy's Special Chicken Salad. Not many people have eat this before."

"Why'd you make three plates?"

"You don't know how to cook nothing at all, do you, Biddy?"

Biddy look shamed and started pondering her toes again. "I didn't lie," she say.

"I ain't saying you a liar. I'm saying you ain't no cook."

She shrug and shake her head.

"How you think you gonna cook for that ole lady?"

Her eyes fill up with tears. I sure didn't want her to go into one of her crying, snot-nose jags.

"I got me an idea," I say.

That stop them tears.

"What?"

"We split up our chores, just like Ms. D. say. I'm gonna cook and you gonna clean."

Biddy get all bright and happy for 'bout a minute. "But what about Miss Lizzy?"

"I'm gonna cook for her too — she just ain't gonna know 'bout it." I get the plastic wrap and put it over one of the stuff tomatoes and wrap it 'round the plate tight.

Biddy wad her face in a knot again. "But . . ."

"You gonna tell her you like to cook in your own kitchen and you'll bring food to her."

"But . . ."

"But what?"

"I can't do that. It would be a wrong thing. Like a lie."

"Biddy, it ain't a lie. It's more like our secret."

I give her a hard look until she look down. I'm not going to let this fool girl mess things up for us.

Biddy

Quincy grabbed that plate with one hand. She grabbed my arm with the other. Tugged me down the steps fast as I could go. Quincy was squawking about me doing 'zactly what she told me to do. She hushed up when we got to the back porch. Made like she was knocking. I tapped on the door. "Miss Lizzy?"

She answered quick. "Is that you, Biddy?" Quincy poked me in the back.

"Yes, 'um. I got lunch for you."

She told me to come in. Quincy let go my wrist. She whispered, "Just follow along and let me do most of the talkin'."

Miss Lizzy set at her kitchen table with a cup of tea. I put the plate in front of her.

"That looks wonderful," Miss Lizzy said. "I didn't expect you to start until tomorrow. I wanted you to have time to get settled in."

"We ready for you to taste Biddy's good cooking," Quincy say.

"Well, then, let's see just how well Biddy cooks," Miss Lizzy said. She pulled off the wrapping. "It looks delicious, Biddy. How did you ever learn to cook like this?"

"Her granny taught her," Quincy said quick-like.

My eyes flew open and my mouth jumped open. I knew I looked a fool standing there. I started crying. We wasn't keeping no secret now. We was telling a bald-face lie. "Miss Lizzy, I got to tell you something." Quincy made a snort sound. "Miss Lizzy, if I try cooking for you, you die of the tow-mane. I didn't lie none about cooking. It was a . . ." I didn't know a right word.

"Misunderstanding?" Miss Lizzy said.

"That's it." My stomach feel better, 'cause Miss Lizzy didn't look mad. "But Quincy here, she can cook. She made this." I pointed down to her pretty tomato-flower.

"Well, then, let's see how it tastes," Miss Lizzy said.

Quincy glare at me, but I don't care. I'm glad we don't have to start things off with a lie. "Ain't nobody gonna eat my food off no bare table," Quincy said. She had her puff-up-chicken-snake face on. "Where you keep place mats and silverware?"

Miss Lizzy pointed and Quincy went to digging. She got a white square of material with scoopy kind of edges. It had a napkin that matched. Quincy spread it out on the table. She folded the napkin on the side. She set a knife and fork nextside the plate. "Wait just a minute," she said, then run out the door.

She come back in with a pink flower.

"You got a vase?"

Miss Lizzy smiled. I don't think I ever saw an old lady smile before. She pointed to a cabinet. I looked over where she pointed. The cabinet had a glass front. A little vase that had designs cut in it was in front.

"That one?" I asked.

Miss Lizzy nodded.

I got it out and wiped it with the dishrag. Filled it up with water, then hand it to Quincy.

Quincy stuck her flower in the glass vase. She put it on the table. "That plate don't quite go with that place mat, but I'm gonna call it good for now."

Miss Lizzy said Quincy was a wonder and we should drink tea while she sampled the salad.

We shook our heads no. Quincy chewed on her bottom lip. Like she was worried as me to see if Miss Lizzy liked her food. I tug the buttons on my coat.

Miss Lizzy got her fork and smiled. Then dip it lady-style in the chicken. We watched her nibble. We watched while she put her fork in the tomato. She got her a big forkful. She ate more. We watched when she closed her eyes, like to say "Amen."

"Quincy, do I taste blue cheese in here?"

Quincy nodded.

I didn't see nothing blue.

"And basil?" Miss Lizzy asked.

Quincy nodded again.

Miss Lizzy said Quincy was "a find," and whoever taught her cooking should be "claimed a saint."

I didn't understand. I could see Quincy didn't either.

"This is the best, most original chicken salad I've ever had the pleasure of tasting."

That's 'zactly what Miss Lizzy said.

Quincy

I thought that fool had done it for sure. Gonna get us flung right out that 'partment by telling she couldn't cook. But my chicken salad done won the day. Don't know why I got edgy 'bout it.

"Did someone teach you to cook?"

I nod at the ole lady. "In the foster home before last. My foster father did sumpin' with computers. He stay home and did housework and cooking. He taught me." I took a pause. "I'm mixed race, in case you wonderin', but I live with white peoples before. You ain't the only one." I said it like a dare. Like she shouldn't expect me to be treat her special.

She nod and use her knife to cut up the tomato.

Ole lady didn't take my dare, and I easy myself down a little. "My foster father taught me all the words in recipes and show me what herbs to use when. He even made up his own recipes. This one of 'em."

"Tell me more," she say.

"Not much more," I said. "My foster mama got a big job in Washington, DC, and they move. I went to another home. Mr. Hallis made me a cookbook of his recipes. I did all the cooking in my last house too. Neither one of them foster parents could cook a lick."

The ole lady finish her lunch and lay her knife 'crosst the edge of her plate. "If you girls are happy with the arrangement, I'm glad to have Quincy cook instead of Biddy." She crook up the corners of her mouth. "I think I'd like to avoid ptomaine." She pet Biddy's hand, so I guess she was funning with her. "Please feel free to use the garden for yourselves, as I've offered before, and, Quincy, please use whatever you need in the kitchen."

I didn't like the idea of being in that ole woman's house, but the idea of cooking in that kitchen sure was fine.

"I ain't calling you Miss Lizzy," I say, the dare back on my tongue.

"Ah," she says. "Makes you feel subservient?"

I don't know what that mean for nothing.

"Slaves called their owners Miss, did they not?" she say.

That ole lady smart.

"I think you could call me Liz. My friends do."

I make my eyes slitty.

She smile, almost sad-like. "Oh, I see. Well, then, would Elizabeth do?"

I nod. She nod back. I guess we done us a deal.

Biddy

I always pondered 'bout Quincy. What color she was. She got real light skin and green eyes. She told Miss Lizzy she was mix-up race.

Quincy

We get things straight with Lizabeth and tromp on upstairs to eat our lunch. Biddy tuck into that chicken salad stuff tomato like a backhoe. She polish it off in about five bites. I don't think that girl ever had good food in her life.

She mop her face up with the napkin, then scrunch her eyebrows together like she was studying on sumpin'. "Which one of your folks was mix-up?" she say, staring at me like I was whole tree full of owls. I was 'bout to reach 'crosst that table and snatch her bald-headed when I saw that the fool wasn't trying to be mean. She just that dumb. I let me out a big ole sigh and tuck my mad down in my pocket.

"My grandma was white and my grandpa black. My mama has pretty light skin. My daddy was white and Mexican and he had green eyes."

Biddy scrunch her eyebrows up a little tighter. "Don't that make you mostly white?"

I hee-hawed then. "Girlfriend, in this part of Texas, if you a little bit black, you all black."

She look like she understand. "I'll clean up our kitchen. I like it sparkledy."

I had tole her a little bit of a lie. When you as light skin as me and usually live with at least one white person, blacks don't want no part of you either. And when you "challenged" and ugly, it pretty much makes no never mind what else you are. You ain't much of nothing.

Biddy

Girlfriend. Quincy called me friend.

Quincy

It be strange. I started making journal tapes for a reading assignment. But here I am, graduated, and I still do it. Some of it because Biddy started doing it and I was wadded-in-a-knot mad—I wanted to make sure mine was better. More tapes and such. But now I like it. It's like I cain't go to sleep until I say my words out loud on the tape. It helps me sort out my head, get things in they right place. I think Biddy feels some such when she clean them cabinets.

I'm feeling strange about Biddy. She ain't like I thought she'd be. Like I said before, she seem like a new-laid egg, but at school, all the boys say they done her. Say she go with anybody. The girls all call her ho. Everybody know she had a baby. I don't want men troubles comin' in our direction. Her and me gonna have a "Come to Jesus" meeting tomorrow.

Biddy

I can hear Quincy talking into her tape. In her bedroom. I do it too. She don't know why, though. This
little tape is something I tell secrets to. Secrets like,
today I'm so happy I could bust. I don't have to cook,
but I'm gonna be eating real good. I get to do for a old
lady that's clean, and she don't holler and call me names.
Sometimes she smiles. I never did know old people was
like that.

I got somebody call me a friend. Nobody ever called
me friend. All kind of new stuff happened to me in one
day. More good than ever happened to me ever. And
even more good—I don't got to go in the world, see
other folks. I cross a little yard. The only peoples I see
are . . . safe. Ain't no boys to trick me and say things.
Ain't nobody calling me ho.

Quincy

I was sleepin' like a lamb in soft straw when I heard the most gosh-awful screamin'. Sound like sumpin' bein' killed in the next room. I haul out my bed and slap on my light.

The screamin' was comin' from Biddy's room.

Had somebody got in our little 'partment?

I grab a big knife in the kitchen and kick open her door.

"I got a knife!"

Biddy was thrashin' and twistin' on her bed, but when I yell out, she scream again and sit up.

I turnt on her overhead light and look around. Weren't nothing in that little bit of a room but a bed and a fat, scared white girl.

"Did you see 'em?" Biddy said.

"Who?"

Biddy look 'round all wild-eyed. Then I swear, she push down her cover and pull up her T-shirt and scrabble at her panties like she checkin' to see that she got 'em on. Then she let out a big sigh.

I seen I still was holding that knife up like I was going to stab somebody, so I let it down. "You screamin' 'cause you think you wet the bed?"

Biddy put her fists up to her eyes and cry like a little child. Somewhere in there, she say, "They not here. I dreamed 'em. They not here."

It was like she was tryin' to make her ownself believe it.

I didn't know what to think. But I knew one thing. That girl was plumb scared to death.

Biddy

Quincy didn't holler at me for waking her up. She ask if I wet the bed. I told her I don't pee my pants. I am scaredy of the dark. Quincy said, "Fool, get you a night-light or keep the hall light on."

"But that runs up the 'lectricity. Granny said so," I told her.

Quincy roll her eyes up in her head. "You paying the bills now, not Granny."

"I can keep me a light on? So there's no dark places in my room?"

"Long as you don't mess around in my room, you can light this whole apartment up." Quincy shook her head. "Guess as long as nothing needs killin', I'll put this knife back in the kitchen."

She left the hall light on. And her door open.

Quincy

When I wake up, I went over to Lizabeth's house to fix breakfast. I stir up some oatmeal and found oranges and a juicer. I made the fresh juice, brew a pot of tea, and cut pears and apples and mix 'em with red grapes. I squeeze a little orange juice over the fruit. Then I made coffee. I like me some coffee in the morning. I put a blue-and-red-plaid tablecloth on the kitchen table and found white dishes with a blue stripe 'round the edges. I set 'em on the table with a white linen napkin. I run outside to pick a couple of daisy flowers I saw blooming in the side yard and 'range 'em in the skinny glass vase.

I didn't have to call Lizabeth. She must heard me rattling 'round, and she thump in with her walker. She smile when she saw the table looking bright and purty. "Where's your places?"

I give her my "Huh?" face.

"There's no reason for you and Biddy to carry your food to your apartment. Please join me for breakfast."

I didn't understand this ole woman. Why she want two Speddies, ones she don't know for boo or squat, sitting at her breakfast table? We just the hired help.

Biddy poke her big face in the back door.

"You're just in time," Lizabeth say. "Quincy is setting your places."

Biddy smile like she pleased as punch. She come in wearing her nasty ole coat. "G'morning, Miss Lizzy. I'm ready to clean this place up proud."

I don't know what else to do, so I set two more places at the table and put out the food. Biddy help Lizabeth settle in her chair.

"Doesn't this look good," Lizabeth say.

"I didn't know if you want tea or coffee, so I made both," I say kinda low-like.

"I drink tea. I keep coffee in case I have a guest that likes it."

I stay husht. I ain't never been no guest.

She smile at us and sip her orange juice. Lizabeth start talking 'bout I can put coffee on her grocery list. And she say she would buy the food for all our meals. I open my mouth to squawk, but she turnt to look at me and said, "Is that all right with you, Quincy? I don't want to offend you with this offer."

She give me a "You know what I mean" look. It wasn't no charity. It was a bonus for my good cooking. I snap my mouth shut.

Biddy was 'bout finished with her oatmeal and eyeing the fruit like it drop down from Mars. "I always have cookies and a Pepsi for breakfast."

43

"And I usually have a piece of toast, so this is a treat for both of us," Lizabeth said. She pet Biddy's hand and Biddy glow.

Lizabeth say we'd have to work us out some menus. She say she has her groceries delivered and she would do the ordering. She ask can I bring home the fresh stuff from the Brown Cow.

I nod.

"Thank you," Lizabeth say.

"Ain't nothing big," I say back.

Biddy give me her "Cain't you be nice to nobody?" look. If that fool think somebody saying thank you mean they like you, she need to smarten up. But she been needing to smarten up since she was borned.

Then Lizabeth said, "Quincy, you can take the vegetables you like from the garden, or you can make a list and Stephen can make a basket for you on the days that he comes here."

I guess Biddy didn't hear, because she was still smilin', but I got all wadded up in a worry knot. Who was Stephen?

Lizabeth tole Biddy they could set up a schedule for what need doing in the house.

Biddy nod, all happy, and set her spoon to flashing in the fruit.

"Mercy, this is good," she say. "I never saw fruit all mix up together like this."

"You eat what I be cookin', 'stead of junk, you gonna lose that ole rhino hino," I say. Even I thought my mouth sound snappish.

"Quincy." Lizabeth said it soft, but it husht and shame me. Then she tole Biddy that she need to have good nutrition and I didn't mean to sound so "harsh." I guess "harsh" the same as mean. She tole Biddy I was right, and eating my good food would make her lose weight. And then she say, "Biddy, won't you be pretty as a picture?"

Woo, I sure didn't expect what came next. Biddy slap her spoon down and reach in her jacket and jerk out a bag of cookies. She start stuffing cookies in her mouth fast as she could chew. "No!" she yell, and bust out in tears. Bawling her lungs out and stuffing those cookies in at the same time. She shove back and run right out that kitchen.

Biddy

Everything was nice till Miss Lizzy said that I was gonna be pretty. Pretty is what made it happen. I can still hear 'em whispering in my ear. "You so pretty. You body so fine. You so hot, baby." I hear 'em in the night. I hear 'em every time a boy look at me.

Quincy

Lizabeth and me stare at one another. I open my mouth to say sumpin' and she raise her bony claw hand up like a traffic cop. I shut my mouth and sull up.

"Go on to work, Quincy. And don't say anything to Biddy. I'll take care of it."

Sure. Dumb, mean Speddie only good enough to cook. Not smart enough to do much else. I know what she thinkin'. She don't fool me with her smiling and inviting and thank-yous.

I slap out the kitchen and stomp on up our stairs. I hear Biddy in her room, blubbering into her tape maybe. I get my clothes and head for the shower-closet, and I hear Lizabeth call up from the bottom of the stairs.

"Biddy, you've neglected to clean the kitchen. In fact, I want all the kitchen cabinets cleaned. Could you think about tackling that today?"

I hear Biddy punch her tape off and clomp to the stairs. "You mean, take out all the dishes and such?" She snuff her nose sumpin' awful.

"Yes, I missed spring cleaning. I'd appreciate a good top-to-bottom clean of this whole place. Starting with the kitchen."

I wait by the bathroom door until Biddy turnt around. Her face was red and her eyes were swole but she stopped bawlin'. Lizabeth already figured out the one thing that would make Biddy feel better. Cleaning out dirt.

Biddy

I got on over to Miss Lizzy's. Pushed up my sleeves. She sat in the kitchen with me. She told me which cabinets she wanted clean. First was the pots and pans cabinets. Some pans was orangey color. They hung on a big round rack from the ceiling. I stacked all the pots and pans on the counters. I got me a bucket with cleaner and water. Scrubbed the cabinet out good. I filled the sink with soapy water. I washed and dried each pot. I tucked it back in its place.

I got four cabinets done. Lunchtime come.

Miss Lizzy had canned stew in the pantry. I knew how to fix that OK. I heat it up. I got crackers. I thought how Quincy made the table look pretty. I shook out the tablecloth from breakfast. I got fresh napkins, bowls, and spoons. Miss Lizzy told me which side for the napkin and spoon. I plunked the crackers on the table in the box. Miss Lizzy didn't say nothing. But I know it didn't look right. I snatched the box back up.

"There's a lovely plate right above the bowls that might look nice for crackers," Miss Lizzy said.

We ate stew. Miss Lizzy talked. "Tell me about yourself, Biddy. Ms. Delamino said that you lived with your grandmother."

"Yes, 'um."

"And your mother is still living?"

"Yes, 'um. But she don't want me."

Miss Lizzy reach out and squeeze my hand. "Life can be cruel sometimes, can't it, Biddy?"

All my life, Granny told me that my mama left me behind because I was worthless. And teachers said my mama must love me very much, but felt she couldn't give me a good life. I might be moderate retardation, but I ain't dumb enough to believe neither.

And I for sure know what cruel means. Miss Lizzy made me feel like a regular person when she said that. She didn't spout me no lies. She said a true thing. Life be cruel. Peoples be cruel sometimes too. I wonder how Miss Lizzy know that as good as me.

Quincy

Biddy went on down to Lizabeth. I took me a shower and dressed in the brown pants and white shirt the Brown Cow give me to wear in the store. I hear Ms. D. honk, and I left to start work at my new job.

Ms. D. introduce me to the store manager. He give me papers to sign, and Ms. D. tole me what all they mean. I sign and we go meet the lady bakery workers. The bakery ain't just a bakery; it has all kind of food. Salads and roast chickens and vegetables and soups and such. One of the ladies tell me and Ms. D. that I'm gonna be doin' "prep" for now. She start explaining, but I stop her talking by saying, "You want me chopping the onions and celery and measuring out the ingredients and such as that."

The lady cut a look at Ms. D., then she say I was right. She hand me an apron and point to a chopping table. Ms. D. tap me on the shoulder and kind of nudge me into a little corner. "Quincy," she say close to my ear. "Try to be friendlier to these women. Don't interrupt when someone is giving you instructions."

"That woman think I'm stupid," I say.

"Quincy, not every word a person says is an insult. Try not to fight the world and everybody in it."

Ms. D. work with Speddies, but she ain't one and don't know what it like. I flap the apron out and work at tyin' it 'round my waist. I didn't look at Ms. D. Then she step up and hug me 'round my shoulders. I stiff up and tears sting my eyes. I don't like touching, that's all.

Ms. D. sigh and say, "Good luck, Quincy." Then she left.

I look up at the lady. "You want these onions chop, dice, or mince?"

Biddy

After lunch, Miss Lizzy said I can have time to myself while she take a nap. Then we'll do her exercise. Miss Lizzy told me her inside ear make her balance bad. That's why she use her walker — so she don't get dizzy and tump over. To help her get better, she does exercise. But she needs me to help her tie cheese. I didn't say nothing. If Miss Lizzy think tying cheese will help her not be dizzy, then I'll help her tie cheese.

Quincy

I cut and chop and mince and dice and mix most of the morning, then I clean and sort stuff in the back. The work ladies, Ellen and Jen, tole me I was a good worker. Like that surprise me.

I got some potatoes, leeks, cream, and a loaf of fresh French bread that been teasin' my nose all day, charge them to Lizabeth, and head for home.

The sacker with a long, greasy ponytail and skinny little beard look me over when I was checking out and made a snort in his nose.

"They shore hiring 'em ugly lately," he said.

Shoot-a-goose, I be used to hearing stuff about my face. I pick up my sack and say, cool as you please, "Look like they hired 'em ugly before me too."

His neck turn red and he look at me real mean. "Bitch," he say, real low, but he say it with a pop. It make me feel like he wanted to bite a hunk out of me. He had that evil face that Mama's boyfriend had right before he grabbed up that brick.

I turnt around and hurried out the store. Once I put enough geography between me and the store, I forgot that boy a little bit. I couldn't let somebody scare me on my first day. When I got to the 'partment, Biddy was talking into her tape with door closed. I change clothes and took the groceries to Lizabeth's. That girl been a cleaning fool. It was clean this morning, but now that kitchen sparkle and smell like—umm, sort of—a cool day after a rain shower. I couldn't get a oven or a floor that clean if I work two weeks. The girl got herself a talent.

I peel the potatoes and set 'em to boil, rub a wood bowl with garlic, mix up a salad, and slice my French bread. I set the table purty, and when the potatoes ready, I finish the soup and call the hogs to the trough.

Biddy help Lizabeth to her chair, and they dip they spoons into the soup.

"There's grass in mine," Biddy say.

"Fool," I say. "That's a parsley sprig. It's call a garnish. You don't got to eat it."

"What's it for, then?"

I roll my eyes up and Lizabeth say, "It's to make the soup attractive and give it a bit of extra flavor, Biddy. And, it shows us that Quincy sees her cooking as an art and that she's proud of it."

I squint my eyes, trying to study if Lizabeth be making fun of me. Too soon to tell.

"Quincy," Lizabeth said, "this is a lovely soup and it's so smooth."

"I run the potatoes and the cream through the blender before I add it to the white sauce in the pot," I say. "I don't like no chunks of potato lumping 'round in my soup."

"Yes, I prefer it this way too. It's wonderful."

Biddy was lapping her soup and using her spoon like a shovel.

Lizabeth look at Biddy, then over at me. She say this was a meal like a princess would eat, and we ought to pretend we in long dresses at a fancy dinner and use "company manners."

Biddy look up with her mouth open and half full of soup.

Lizabeth talk on 'bout a princess would sit with her back straight and on the front of the chair. Lizabeth was already like that. Biddy hitch up her back and waggle her big ole butt forward.

Lizabeth pick up her spoon and say that a princess hold her spoon pretty and dip it in the soup, and a princess would spoon away from her body. Then she dip her spoon into her soup and held the spoon up. Biddy turnt her grip on the spoon so that she wasn't holding it in her fist, but on her fingers, and spoon her soup just like Lizabeth did.

"And a princess brings the spoon to her mouth, not her mouth to the spoon," Lizabeth tole her. Biddy tried. Her head kept pulling down to the bowl, and she look like one of them toys that duck in and out of a water glass. When she finally got how to keep her head up, the soup slop off the spoon.

"A princess fills her spoon half full so she can take dainty princess sips."

A smile march right 'crosst Biddy's face. She try the whole thing again, and this time got her some soup into her mouth.

Lizabeth kept up her chatter, showing how a princess would use a salad fork and how to break the bread into little pieces rather than tear at a whole slice with her teeths. Biddy was having herself a high ole time pretending she be some kind of fancy lady.

I got me good table manners. Mr. Hallis show me all that when he taught me cooking. He didn't talk no stuff 'bout no princess.

Biddy

I ain't White Trash. Miss Lizzy said I'm a princess. And a princess don't wear a coat full-up with food. I'm going to push it in nextside the hangers at the back of my closet. I'll just wear it if I have to go in the world.

Quincy

We went back to our little apartment and I tole Biddy we need to have us a talk. She nod her head and plop down on the couch. More like she set perched on it with a straight back, like Lizabeth just taught her. Got to admit, the girl hold tight to things oncet she learn 'em.

"Biddy, we got to have us some rules."

Biddy nod again. She even got that Lizabeth smile on her face.

"It's about menfolk."

That smile drop off her face like — I don't know the word, but like you drop a rock into a bucket.

"Menfolks?"

"See, the whole world know about you and menfolk. What you do with men is your bidness — but I got me a right not to want 'em 'round here." I point to the dent in my head. "Sometimes folk get hurt from other people's men hanging around."

Biddy surprise me then. She didn't start no crying or snatch up a cleaning rag. Her look sat with a backbone inside it.

"Quincy, when you see me with boys or menfolk?"

My mouth open, but my words seize up. I thought hard a minute. Since seventh grade, I ain't never seen Biddy having no truck with boys. They call her names, but she don't talk to none of them. In fact, she don't even look at any kind of man. My brain got addled.

"I guess I hasn't." I kind of jut out my chin and sound mad, so she don't think I'm wrong or nothing.

Biddy stand up. "Well, then." And she turnt her back and walk off into her bedroom and shut the door.

Biddy

Seems to me, other peoples in this world got as much trouble learning as I do.

Quincy

Biddy march off to her room and shut her door. Left me there with my mouth hanging. Back in school with people watching or poking at her, Biddy would have thrown some kind of fit, or get her feelings hurt and run off crying. But after Lizabeth tell her she a princess, just one little time, Biddy be a whole 'nother person. It like she and Lizabeth be some kind of team together.

I stomp off to my room, but thinking 'bout Biddy's straight princess back and how Lizabeth pet Biddy's hand and be all gooey with her piss me plumb off. I slammed my door hard enough for Biddy to hear.

I thump down on my bed. My clock say it just six thirty. I ain't got no new comic to read. We don't got a TV. What I'm supposed to do? Knit like some ole lady? I don't know how to knit, and who need a sweater in Texas?

Then it catch up to me. It ain't just seein' Biddy with boys. Everybody know she a ho because she done had that baby. Biddy got me all confused talking about not seein' her with no boys and acting like a princess and . . . now I feel like snatching somebody's head off they neck—that's what I feel like doing.

That's what I'll do. I got up and put me on some shorts and working shirt and went downstairs to the little garden. I worked me up a sweat yanking weeds.

After I work some of the mad off, I look up and see Lizabeth standing on her porch.

"Quincy, I've made iced tea. You look like you could use a drink."

I didn't want to sit and drink tea with Biddy's best friend. "I want to get the rest of the garden clear of these weeds. Sun's 'bout to go down." I kept yanking. Little harder maybe.

"The young man that cuts the grass and does the flower beds weeds the garden for me. You don't need to do that."

Lizabeth put the tea down on a little table on the back porch. She go inside and come back out with another glass of tea. She sit down in a curly metal chair by the table and took a drink of her tea.

"I know you like to do things your own way," she say. "But you're taking a job that someone else needs to support his father right now. Please come join me."

I sigh. I hate that ole lady for being smart. I should have just gone back inside as soon as I seen her. I wipe my hands on the back of my shorts and go up to her porch. I sat down and sip the tea. It was cool and sweet.

"Who is Stephen? He the one that weeds and cut the grass?" I asked.

"Yes, he comes by about every other day to attend to something or another around here. His father was my gardener before, but he's ill and his son has taken his place. He's not much older than you and Biddy, I think."

"You gonna have a problem."

"What? I don't understand."

"Biddy gots problems with boys; let's just leave it at that."

Lizabeth's face got all in a bunch, then it went all kind of wide when her eyes open out big. "Oh, I never considered . . ." She took a sip of her tea. "Stephen is a lovely young man. Biddy will understand when she meets him that he . . ." She look at me and pushed at her hair and her voice change.

"I remember being young and strong like you," Lizabeth say. "My balance problems have made me old before my time. And I hate it."

I didn't know what that meant for nothing. It must have showed, because Lizabeth said, "You think I'm very old, don't you? I'm only sixty-two."

Sixty-two, that's old as dirt. Some grandmas ain't much past forty.

Lizabeth must have seen the look on my face real good then. 'Cause she laugh. At first I thought she was laughing at me. But I couldn't get mad 'cause her laugh was all—I don't know a word, but her laugh rolled around like puppies. Some kind of way it made me laugh, just a little.

Lizabeth shook her head and kind of hummed to herself. Sip her tea. "Quincy, I won't see it in the mirror, but you just told me. I'm an old woman." She sip her tea again and sigh. "Now, when did that happen?" She didn't say that to me.

I kept on saying nothing. I might be drinking iced tea with a crazy woman.

I just been out of school a few days, and I got the Buffalo-Butt Princess hiding in her room and the Laughing-at-Nothing Ole Lady here on the porch.

Living on my own is nothing like I thought.

Biddy

I look out my little window and I see Quincy and Miss Lizzy drinking ice tea and laughing.

I get a sad feeling. I wonder if they're talking about me. Laughing about dumb, fat Biddy.

Does Quincy call Miss Lizzy girlfriend?

Quincy

I was wondering, should I tell Biddy 'bout this Stephen this morning before we go down to breakfast or let Lizabeth do it? I didn't have to think about it too long 'cause just then I hear a lawn mower.

I go and tap Biddy's door. "Biddy, I gots to come in and talk to you."

Biddy open her door. "What's that ruckus? Is that a lawn mower? Who's mowing the lawn?" Biddy start toward the window.

I catch holt of her wrist and swing her back around. "That's what I got to tell you. Lizabeth gots a boy, or a man — well, he 'bout our age — that work for her doing the garden. His name is Stephen."

That ole fool runt to her closet and snatch that coat. It still had cookies and candies all pin in it like she be a walking snack machine. Her face go even more ashy than before, and her eyes go plumb wild. If I didn't know better, I'd say that she was afraid.

"Quincy, I don't feel so good. I don't think I'll have breakfast this morning."

"What are you talking about? Take off that coat. It's summertime."

"Maybe when that boy is mowing the front I'll come over," Biddy say, and I could see a cryin' jag about to commence.

"Biddy, what are you worried about? He ain't gonna hurt you."

"Boys look at me dirty. They say dirty things and they laugh. They do things."

I didn't know exactly what she meant by that, but I had me a bad feelin'. "OK, you stay here until he mows the front and then you come over. I'll tell Lizabeth you not hungry."

I went to work, my head still trying to sort itself out. I punch my time card in the computer like they showed and went to fetch my apron.

"Well, if it ain't Butt Ugly."

That boy from yesterday.

"My name is Quincy."

"My name is Robert. You need to say it real nice." His eyes were gone slitty, and his words slid through his teeths just like the devil his ownself would talk.

He stood between me and the aprons. "I need to get me an apron." I reach my arm out past him.

He grab my wrist. "Say 'please.'" He step in close to

me and turn my arm up so it hurt. He was close enough I could feel his breaths on my cheek. "Say 'pretty please.'"

"You let me go." I say it loud, but my insides shake.

"Not until you say 'please.' Not until you beg me nice."

I jerk my arm, and he twist it up harder. He push me back 'gainst the wall and push himself hard against me.

"Quincy?"

Jen come into the little room. Robert drop my arm quick-like and step back.

"What's going on in here?"

"We're just getting acquainted," Robert say.

I shook my arm and rub where he had helt it. There was too many things just then and too many people and I couldn't think what was what. I step past Robert and grab an apron. Then something inside me clutch up and I turnt back to Jen. I wisht I had Biddy's coat. "That boy call me names and grab my arm. I want him to stay away from me."

Jen's face got red. "Robert," she say.

"That ugly bitch is lyin'," he say. "She come on to me. She's just a lyin' ho, trying to get me in trouble."

I couldn't believe it! That boy call me a ho! These folk didn't know me. They might believe him.

"That ain't how it happen'," I yell. "I ain't no ho, and I didn't . . ."

"Quiet, both of you," Jen say. "Let's go see the manager."

Jen take us to the manager's office. I tell my story and Robert tell his lies. Then the manager axt me to get on to work and leave Robert with him.

I went to my work. Jen pull me into the back. "Did that boy hurt you? You know what I mean? Did he . . . ?" She stop and look kind of embarrassed. "Did he touch you?"

" 'Course he touch me. I tole you he grab holt of my arm."

Jen made a face. "Quincy, not like that. Did he 'touch' you?"

I get it. "No, not like that." I don't know why I didn't say he push himself against me. I know Jen had seen that.

"He's a bad one, Quincy, and he's been in trouble here before. Stay away from him."

"I ain't no ho. I don't want no truck with him."

"I believe you," Jen say. But her face say different.

The manager's door bang shut. Robert stomp out yelling.

"I don't need this crappy job. I had enough of this shit."

He jerk his apron and throw it on the ground and come up to my counter. He look hard and point his finger straight at my face. He didn't say nothing. He just stare at me and jab his finger, then snap his thumb like he firing a gun at me. He charge on out the door.

"Good riddance," Ellen, the bakery lady, say.

Jen give me a look I didn't understand. Like she thought I stole sumpin'.

I got me a knife and chop celery. My hand shake only at first.

Biddy

Why did some boy name Stephen have to come ruin everything? I might could learn to cut grass. I can pull weeds. He don't need to be here.

I peek out the window at him. He's not looking toward me. I just hear the mower in the front of the house. I skedaddle down the steps crosst the yard to Miss Lizzy's.

I clean the kitchen up nice, then I get to work making the bathroom sparkledy.

I was just starting to feel all right when Miss Lizzy asks could I come make some iced tea and meet Stephen. I turn around. A sweaty boy stand behind me in the doorway. I must of turn white as a ghost. I kind of yelp.

He smile and say, "I didn't mean to scare you." And he smile.

I don't like no boys to smile at me.

I back against the sink. Looking for a place to run out that kitchen. But Miss Lizzy standing there in her walker between me and the door. I couldn't run her over.

I took some gulping big breaths. I saw that Miss Lizzy and that boy was looking at me like I gone crazy. I tried to think hard. This wasn't no barn. And Miss Lizzy was right here. I might was going to be all right. I slid with my back still to the counter so I didn't have to turn away from the boy. I got the tea. I slid along. Fetched a glass. Slid some more. I came to the fridge. I got some ice. I kept my eyes on him all the while. Then I thump the glass of tea on the table. While I was doing all this, Miss Lizzy was talking.

"Biddy, this is Stephen. He is in charge of the gardening. He does other landscaping jobs too, but he's our regular gardener and will be here parts of the day often. Stephen, this is Biddy. She takes care of the house and of me when I need it. She's a great help."

That boy stuck his hand out and say, "Glad to make your acquaintance, Biddy."

I didn't know what no "quaintance" was. But I for sure wasn't going to touch his hand. I push back harder again' the counter till I was almost bending backwards. He looked at me kinda sad-like. He took his hand back out the air.

"I've known Stephen since he was practically a puppy," Miss Lizzy said. "His father was my gardener before, and Stephen used to come help out. He's a fine young man, Biddy."

"Thank you, Miss Elizabeth. That's kind of you to

say." That boy picked up his glass and kind of tilted it toward Miss Lizzy. "If you don't mind, I'll take this outside to drink. I need to get the front mowed before the day heats up."

Miss Lizzy say something to him, and then he nod to me and say, "Good-bye, Biddy. I hope to see you again sometime." I didn't say nothing. I didn't move.

He left outside the front door. I could breathe inside my chest again. I felt like I might fall in a heap on the ground. My legs felt so squishy.

"Biddy," Miss Lizzy say. "Stephen is a nice boy. He would never hurt you. Has a boy ever hurt you, Biddy? Is that why you were so afraid of him?"

Miss Lizzy can't know my secrets. She won't never let me live in her princess house no more. "I ain't scaredy. I just don't mess with no boys. That's all." I went back to scrubbing my pots.

Quincy

All afternoon, people looking at me like I done sumpin' wrong. Hard to believe Biddy didn't take a whipping stick to folks that look at her that way all the time. But then, Biddy, she done sumpin' with them boys. I mean, I know sumpin' gots done. I'm thinkin', maybe, since she seem so scared of boys . . . I don't know what I'm thinkin'. All I know is I didn't do nothing but try to get my apron.

I wonder if Biddy done met Stephen or if she was able to keep shut of him all day. I shake my head and wonder why I care what ole Buffalo Butt doin' and if she wearin' that raggedy coat. No business of mine.

Biddy

Miss Lizzy call me to help her with her exercise. I found out that Miss Lizzy don't want me to tie no cheese. Tie cheese sound like cheese. But it ain't. It's the name of Miss Lizzy's exercises.

Miss Lizzy come out her room. She wasn't wearing no suit like she done the day we met her. And she wasn't wearing pants and a long shirt that's still real dress-up looking, like she wore yesterday. She had sweatpants and a T-shirt. Miss Lizzy go into a room nextside the living room. Wasn't nothing inside there except a big soft-feeling pallet thing on the floor. And a long pole running alongside one of the walls.

Miss Lizzy say she gonna hold on that "bar" and do her tie cheese. All I had to do was stand close. So if she lose her balance I help her. She say I'm there as a "caution." If she fell doing her exercise while nobody was there, she'd might not could get up. And that would put her in a pickle.

I nod my head like this make sense. Cheese wasn't cheese, so I don't guess she means she really get put inside a pickle.

Miss Lizzy put her walker by the door. She go onto that mat and hold on the sideways pole for a minute. Then she lift up her arms and look like she was holding a big watermelon in front of her stomach. "This is centering the chi," Miss Lizzy say. I listened. She didn't say "cheese." She leave off the end and just say "chee."

Then she done other stuff. About holding up the heavens. Breaking up waves. And holding back the tiger. Little silver-headed lady putting her hands out funny and kinda squatting don't look like she's holding back a tiger. But Miss Lizzy was already talking about dragon dance or dragon stand or something. I watch and listen. Wait to see if she was going to tump over.

She get done and said she need to put her hand on my shoulder so she could get to her walker.

"Thank you, Biddy. Have you ever seen anyone do tai chi before?"

I shake my head.

Miss Lizzy laugh. Not a big laugh like with Quincy. "It must seem odd to you, then?"

I don't know what "odd" mean.

Miss Lizzy look at my face. "'Odd' means strange, puzzling. It's odd that a little old lady waves her arms around like a crazy person." She laugh again like she was inviting me to laugh with her.

I laugh back. Now Miss Lizzy done laugh twice. I don't feel bad now.

Then there was a knock on the back door.

"That will be Stephen, I think," Miss Lizzy say. "Will you get that, Biddy?"

I go to the door all scaredy. But Miss Lizzy coming along behind me. So it's probly all OK. I open the door and Stephen's smiling real big. "You two wanna see something pretty?"

Quincy

I chop and mix and did my job without talking for the rest of my shift. My mind was boiling. These people don't know me and they do know Robert and they know he's no count, but they still be looking at me like . . . well, like people look at Biddy.

I clocked out and left without no good-byes and stomp down the street like I was squashing bugs. That got a little of the mad outta me. I got to Lizabeth's and thought I'd pick a tomato or two and some basil. I head to the garden and, boy, did I see me a sight.

Biddy was lying on her fat stomach, wiggling her fingers at a patch of rosemary and singing. The girl had finally gone insane-crazy.

"Biddy, what you doing wallering in that dirt?"

She poke her head up, smiling big as you please. "Quincy, shush and come see this."

I figure the girl must of found her some candy or sumpin', she was so happy. I squat down. She point to the back of the rosemary. Through the branches I seen sumpin' brown. I squint up my eyes and rock over a little and I saw it. A big old Mama Duck sitting on some eggs.

"How you find this ole duck?"

"Stephen showed us."

"Stephen? He your boyfriend now?" I knew I done wasted my time worryin' 'bout Biddy and being scared of boys. When they gots somethin' she want, she . . .

"Quincy, I'm not going to tell you another time to hush about me and boys. He show this duck to me and to Miss Lizzy." She nod her head in that "I ain't talkin' 'bout this no more" way and turnt back to the duck. I swear I don't understand that girl.

Biddy waggle her fingers closer, and Mama Duck hiss through the hole in her beak and struck her head out like a snake trying to bite Biddy's fingers.

I jump up. "Biddy, you leave that duck alone. It's gonna bite you."

"No, she ain't. She's just being a good mama. Telling me to leave her babies alone."

I couldn't believe this fool girl. "You keep waggling you fingers at that duck, it's gonna bite you a good one. Don't come running to me when you get the duck rabies." I got me tomatoes and basil and left.

Biddy stay outside singing to that duck.

Biddy

I got to get corns and a bowl of water. That way Mama Duck can eat and drink right here. She won't have to leave her babies.

Quincy

Biddy come in whilst I was washing the tomatoes. She grab her a little bowl out the cabinet.

"S'cuse me," she say, kind of singy-songy, and shove her bowl under the water.

"What you doing?"

"I'm taking water to Mama Duck."

I just stare.

"And I need some dry corns. Ducks like dry corns, right?"

"You ever hear me quack?"

Biddy's face knot up. "Huh?"

"I look like a duck? How I'm s'pose to know what a duck eat?"

Biddy look at me like I'm stupid. "You the one knows how to read. If I could read, I'd make sure I learned things."

My head start to ache. I couldn't think of nothing to say. I went back to washing the tomatoes.

"So, can you get me some dry corns at the store where you work?"

"Biddy, I work at a grocery store. I don't know where to get dry corn. And you don't got to go feeding that duck. It's been having babies all by itself for a long time. It don't need your help."

Biddy sniff her nose. "That's what you know."

Now, what was that s'pose to mean?

We went on over to Lizabeth's and I roast us a chicken and made a tomato and basil salad with hunks of cheese and olive oil drizzled on top. Biddy watch how Lizabeth eat and use her napkin and did exactly how Lizabeth did.

"Miss Lizzy, do you know where I can get dry corns?" Biddy axt.

"Oh, Lord, here we go," I say.

Biddy cut me a look and say, "You hush. You don't even like ducks."

Lizabeth put her napkin up to her mouth. Look like maybe she be hiding a smile. Now Biddy got Lizabeth thinking I'm a fool.

"Ain't got nothing to do with liking or not liking ducks," I said low-like.

"Miss Lizzy, can you get rabies from a duck?"

That napkin too small to hide Lizabeth's smile now.

"Why, Biddy, I'm not sure. I don't think I've ever heard of"—a little laugh jump out Lizabeth's mouth—"duck rabies."

Biddy nod her head at me, like "See!"

"We need to be eating this chicken before it get cold," I say. I say it loud so Biddy would hush her mouth.

"Miss Lizzy, I need corns to feed that Mama Duck so she don't leave her babies."

A look crosst Lizabeth's face that was so sad and soft I was certain sure right then that Lizabeth knew 'bout Biddy's took-away baby.

"You could ask Stephen to get you some corn."

"I can't be asking no boy for nothin'," Biddy say, so low I almost couldn't hear her.

Lizabeth let the clock ticktock a little bit, then say, "I believe you could buy dry corn at a feed store, Biddy."

"I have to leave here and go get it?" Biddy slunk down. But right away she hitch up her back. "How far is a feed store?"

"We'd have to look it up. We'll do that another time. As Quincy said, we need to eat this wonderful chicken before it gets cold."

I thought about saying we oughta roast that duck and make omelets from the eggs, but sassy as Biddy done got, I figured she might stab me with her fork. Fool girl acting so crazy she might have the duck rabies already.

Biddy

I'm going to do it! I'm going to find a feed store and I'm going to walk to it and buy dry corns. I don't care what Quincy got to say.

Quincy

I had me a bad dream last night. Inside my head, Robert jabbing his finger at me. I be seeing the look in his eyes and Jen saying, "He's trouble, he's trouble, he's trouble." I hope I'm just havin' crazy bad dreams like Biddy and didn't go get the second sight all of a sudden.

I woke up tired after all my dreaming. I had me a long hot shower and went to Lizabeth's. I drank extra-strong coffee whilst I made us omelets and toast.

Biddy bustle in just about the time Lizabeth show up. Lizabeth look a bit peckish. I wondered what kind of dreams she had. Biddy was nervous and rattling the silverware until Lizabeth and me both got a case of the jumps. All three of us did a lot of egg poking, and more food got scooted around than ate.

"Biddy, dear, could you please not tap your spoon like that? I have a touch of headache," Lizabeth say.

Biddy drop her spoon with a clatter. "Sorry, Miss Lizzy."

Lizabeth didn't hear her. She was stirring and staring into her tea.

"Miss Lizzy?"

Lizabeth jerked like she been woke up. "Yes?"

"Can you show me where to find a feed store? And tell me how to walk there?"

Lizabeth stare at Biddy with worry and sad all mixed up in her face. "Yes. Let's go do that now. I'm not hungry." She turnt to me. "Everything is wonderful, Quincy. I'm having a bit of a bad day."

Woo, don't I know how that feel.

Those two went off in another room. I left the dishes for Biddy. That was part of the deal. My feet walked slow toward the Brown Cow. Seem like now that Robert was gone, I'd feel better, but I was feeling like a fairy story and the children heading into the dark woods.

Biddy

Miss Lizzy drew a map. She made arrows on the street where I turn. She told me the directions like it was a story so I could remember. "Walk until you see a building that looks like a little cottage and then turn toward it, then go until you see a stop sign and turn the other direction." She gave me money and said it was a "vance" on my salary. I helped Miss Lizzy back to her bed. She asked me to make her herb tea and to turn on the radio real soft.

"You know, Biddy, I was raised to be a southern belle. That means that I always use good manners."

I look at Miss Lizzy. "Why, you got the best manners I ever see. You always dress up nice. Your clothes never got wrinkles—and you don't slurp soup."

Miss Lizzy give a little smile, but she still look sad. "Good manners can mean keeping out of others' personal business. But it also means helping right wrongs."

Miss Lizzy didn't seem to be talking to me. But there wasn't nobody else in the room. "I think of my youngest son often. My boy that died. I've often wondered what kind of man he would have been. How I wish I could see him just once more." She sighed and looked back at me. "Why don't you go get your corn now, Biddy. I need to rest and be alone with my thoughts."

Miss Lizzy had a child that died?

That was worse than having a child being took away.

I worried because Miss Lizzy didn't feel good. But she didn't want me to stay.

I went to our apartment. I studied my map. I got down the stairs partways. I kind of freezed up. I always go across the yard to the big house. Now I would be out on the street with peoples besides Miss Lizzy or Quincy. Boys, maybe.

I tore upstairs. Got my coat and buttoned it up. I could go now.

Quincy

I got to the Brown Cow and, sure 'nuff, there was a ole beat-up car in the parking lot and Robert sitting in the front seat. He hung his arm out the window, and he had a knife. He tap the side of the door with the blade and watch me walk up to the doors. He didn't say nothing, the man in the driver's seat didn't say nothing, but when I pull open the door to the Brown Cow, somebody tap the horn. I jump about a mile and turn around. Robert jab the knife out at me, then make like he slice it sideways. Nothing change in his face. He just kept staring with his eyes all tight and full of mean. Then they tore out the parking lot with the tires squealing.

I went straight to the bathroom and threw up my little bit of breakfast.

Biddy

I studied Miss Lizzy's map. I walked with my head down except when I had to see a turn. If I didn't look at nobody, they couldn't look at me. I got to the feed store. Nothing bad happened.

There was a man at the counter. I hung back at the door, scaredy. But he wasn't no boy. He had white hair. I wasn't scaredy of mens as much as boys. I had to do this for Mama Duck. I took myself up to the counter.

I asked the counter man if ducks eat dry corns. He smiled at me. But not mean or dirty. He say that ducks like corns plenty. I asked for a little sack. Enough to feed a Mama Duck. He made a chuckle, but it was nice. He went off a ways. He came back toting a paper bag.

I pushed my money across the counter. "Is this enough money?"

He looked how peoples do when they figure I'm "challenged."

But he didn't make no fun. He smiled and said, "That's one lucky Mama Duck." He took my money. Rung it up on his cash register. Handed me money back. I turned to leave.

"You be sure to come back and tell me about the baby ducks, you hear?"

I didn't know what to do. I waited, scaredy to hear something mean or bad. But he lifted his hand and made a little wave for me.

I grabbed hold the door. I took me a deep breath and give a fast wave. I got out of there. I was OK to keep my head up all the way home.

Quincy

We been here a week when Ms. D. come by. She sit on our couch and axt how we been. Biddy up and tell Ms. D. 'bout how I'm cooking for Lizabeth first pop out the box. If I could have got my hands 'round her fat neck, I'd have choked her. Ms. D. don't be needing to know our bidness.

Biddy

Ms. Delamino came by to visit our first weekend. She was real nice. I bragged on Quincy's cooking. I swear, instead of pleased, Quincy got all sulled up. I told Ms. Delamino about Mama Duck. She asked to see. She thought it was fine that we had a Mama Duck in our garden. Ms. Delamino said she wanted to talk to Quincy alone. I stayed outside to sing to Mama Duck.

Quincy

Ms. D. come back in without Biddy and sit down. She smile. I figure she gonna tell me I shouldn't be doing Biddy's cooking for her or some such.

"Well," she say, looking pleased as punch. "This is working out just fine."

I give her my "Huh?" look.

"Quincy, we didn't put you and Biddy together just because you happened to graduate at the same time."

I didn't know what to say.

"We spend a lot of time deciding what two people have strengths and weakness that kind of, well, fit with each other."

Ms. D. must see in my face I didn't know what she was talking about.

"How is this arrangement working out for you? If you are doing the cooking for Biddy, what does she do for you in return?"

Ms. D. sat for a while. She wait and didn't say no more. Shoot-a-goose!

"She clean our apartment."

Ms. D. nod. "So, you are learning to cooperate?"

I give her a look.

Ms. D. smile this time. "Get along. Share the work."

"I guess so. But she still Biddy and I still Quincy."

"Quincy," Ms. D. say, "you and Biddy won't find it as easy as most people to live on your own. You'll have to help each other."

"Well, I did help her. I am helpin' her. Does that mean I win somethin'?"

Ms. D.'s smile straighten out. "I hoped you wouldn't keep score."

I follow her out and there's Biddy singing the "Itsy-Bitsy Spider" song to her duck. I plumb weary of that song. I sure wish she knew more.

Biddy

Ms. Delamino tell us that she has both our paychecks. She's taking us to the bank to help us open checking accounts. Then we going on a shopping spree. I don't know exactly what that is. But I think we're going to spend the money we made this week.

The bank was all quiet and scaredy. Ms. Delamino done most of the doing and handed Quincy and me our checkbooks. I take my check. I put it in the bank. Then I get some spending money. Quincy or Ms. Delamino or even Miss Lizzy can help me with the check-writing part.

Then we went off to a big store. I told Ms. Delamino and Quincy that I didn't like those T-shirts that Granny bought me no more. I want to wear dresses, like a princess. But dresses that was OK to do my work in. Quincy said, "Halleluiah!" And, she sort of push me toward a row of dresses. They help me find three dresses they called jumpers. They was made of stuff like blue jeans. Then Quincy push me along to the place where there was pajamas and robes.

"Get you some pj's and a nightie and a robe and some slippers," she said. She took off and Ms. Delamino helped me.

When Quincy came back, she had a shopping bag in her hand, but she didn't tell nobody what she bought.

I was out of money now. Quincy bought her some new shoes to wear at the Brown Cow. Then Ms. Delamino took us out to have lunch at a real restaurant. I showed I learned to eat like a princess.

We came back to our little house. Ms. Delamino said we done just fine our first week.

Later that evening, I went in my room. Sitting on my bed was four night-lights and an alarm clock.

Quincy

Couple of weeks had gone by when Jen tapped me on my shoulder one day at work. I pulled back and give her a dirty look.

"Sorry," she say. "I just thought you'd like to take your break with me. We could talk."

I look over to Sandra. She nod. "It's slow. Y'all go on."

I take off my apron and follow Jen to the break room. She get me a Coke and put it down in front of me. "We haven't had a chance to get to know each other," she say.

I shrug. Ain't nobody done this before. In school all anybody need to know is you in Special Ed.

"You been here more than a while now, and Ellen and me don't know anything but your name." She make a twisty-looking face. "We think you don't like us."

I push my straw up and down through the plastic cap and it make a squawky sound.

Jen tap her fingers on the table. "What did we do to make you mad at us?"

I didn't know what to do. "You know stuff about me." I didn't look up. I kept on squawking my straw.

Jen kind of sighed and pull her paper hat off her head and rub at the place where the elastic make a red mark in her forehead. "You're right. I know that you do your work without complaining. I know that you are fast and neat and clean. And I know that you don't talk much. And you don't seem to like being touched."

I nodded. All that was right. "You left something out. You know I'm a Speddie. I know you got tole I was a special work program."

Jen's face got the red creeps, so I know I done hammered the right nail.

"You're not exactly what I thought," Jen say.

I clonked my cup down. "Right. You 'spected somebody to come in here talking all weirdy—with they mouth all hanging loose and saying they words all 'Duh, duh, duh' kinda like. And you thought I'd look all stupid in my face, so you could just see that I was Special Ed by giving me the eyeball. And you thought, 'Here we go, I'm gonna have tell her a hunert times how to do every little thing and pro'lly have to do it myself anyway—shoot-a-goose, she's so dumb she cain't even live on her own.'" I crost my arms over my chest and lean back in my chair. "That about right?"

Jen rub that red crease in her forehead again. Then

she smile. "That's about right. I didn't expect you to be so, well, normal."

"I ain't normal. I got problems learning. That's what Special Ed means. We all got some kind of dys. It don't mean we need help remembering to breathe in and out."

"Some kind of what?"

"We all got a dys. One kind of dys means you cain't read. Biddy got that kind of dys. I cain't say all the dys words 'cause they long. But I can say mine. Dysgraphia. That dys means I can read a word and know how to spell it, but when my hand goes to write it—it just don't come out." I lift up my chin. "I can write. It's just hard and I'm slow at it."

"Can you do math?"

I tighten my arms crost my chest and tried not to knock that woman plumb silly. She already silly enough. "Yes, I can add, and subtract and multiply and divide. Cain't do much more than that, though. You need somebody to do more math than that back there sorting out the celery and the onions?"

"Nope," Jen say. "I was just hoping you could do math, because Ellen and me flunked math and if we don't have a calculator, we're kind of screwed."

I loosed up my arms a little bit. "I might could help you out," I said. "And if it get busy, I could help you at the register, maybe."

"Mr. Dunne would have to approve, but it works for me," Jen said. She started tucking her hair back under her paper hat.

I get up and throw my cup in the trash. I want to make sure she understand. "Sometimes Speddies got to learn different ways. I live with another Speddie name Biddy, and you cain't just tell her a bunch a stuff straight out. She don't get it or remember it. But if you tell it to her like it's a story—that girl don't never forget."

Jen and me left the break room and walk back to work. "Biddy sounds interesting," Jen say.

"She real different from me," I say. I didn't say what I was thinking. I was thinking about Biddy and that Mama Duck. Difference between Biddy and me was . . . I didn't know 'zactly how to think it, but it was kinda like I think about the outside of stuff and Biddy, she think about the inside.

Biddy

Mama Duck been doing good. She been eating corns. Drinking water. And taking good care of her eggs. She makes sure I don't bother her eggs none. That means she's a good Mama Duck.

That boy Stephen, he don't bother me. He say "Hey" when he see me. But he don't try to give me no candy. He don't try to get me alone in no dark places either. He just tend to his work. I tend to mine. I heard he and Miss Lizzy talk about me. He wondered what he done to scare me so much. That make me feel some kind of bad. But not bad enough to talk to him 'bout it. Quincy give him the evil eye when she see him. That Stephen boy, he kind of sull up around her too. I don't think they will ever be friends together. That's good. If Quincy gonna have a friend, it needs to be me.

Miss Lizzy been fretty. And I think her inside ear is making her dizzier than ever. I had to keep her from tumping over two times. That makes her cranky.

It makes me feel a little bit more easy around Miss Lizzy knowing she can be cranky sometimes. If somebody smiles all the day every day, you know that you ain't the reason. Now when she smile at me, it's kind of like I made a cat purr.

Quincy been in a good enough mood. Except for once she came home from work and she looked scaredy. I never saw Quincy look scaredy before and it made me scaredy too. I asked her what was wrong.

"Biddy, you ever see a ole beat-up-looking car hanging 'round here?"

I told her I didn't. She asked was I sure. Why Quincy afraid of an old car?

Sometimes she'd sit on the little porch and watch the street. She must not saw nothing, because she get in a better mood every time she came in after watching.

Quincy

Lizabeth calls to tell us that she is in bed for the night. Biddy frets that Lizabeth might fall or sumpin'. So she don't get easy till after that phone ring.

When she hanged up, I said, "You worry 'bout that ole lady too much."

"Don't you worry 'bout who I worry 'bout," Biddy say.

Woo, that girl nothing like the one used to cry all the time in school.

"I don't see you worryin' 'bout your ole granny," I say.

Biddy thump down on the couch and get puzzled in her face.

"You don't never call her or go see her," I say.

"She don't got no phone," Biddy say.

"Is it 'cause she was mean to you?"

Biddy sigh. "I thought that's just how it was. Didn't know much different. I know teachers was nice. But Granny said they was paid to be nice."

"So why don't you never go see her?"

Biddy studied me. It was like she couldn't figure out why I didn't understand something so easy.

"Because I live here now," she said.

Biddy

After Quincy go to her room, I thought of something. Her light showed under her door, so I knocked.

"Quincy, you still awake?"

"Cain't sleep with somebody peckin' on my door. What you need?"

I opened the door and Quincy was sitting in bed looking at her cookbook.

"What about all your foster folks?"

"What about 'em?"

"Do you call them? Why don't you ever go see 'em?"

I close my book. "Biddy, some of them fosters was 'bout like your granny. They give me a room and some food 'cause they got a check from the state. And treated me worse than a dog. One family sent me back 'cause they said it wasn't worth the money to have to look at me crosst the supper table."

I didn't know what to do. I stared down at my toes.

"When I got put with Mr. and Mrs. Hallis, I thought I had done gone to heaven. But I'd only been there a little bit past a year when they had to leave. Good don't happen much and it don't stay stuck. My last foster folk was nice. They was good to me. But I knew I didn't have but a year left with them either."

"OK," I said. "But why do you think I should want to go see Granny?"

Quincy picked up her book and opened it. "I never lived in one place with one person, like you. I thought it might be different. That's all. Guess it ain't."

I went to my room. I patted my princess table. Smoothed my bedcovers.

How come Quincy can't see that now is different?

That before we didn't belong nowhere.

And now we belong here.

Quincy

I got up one Satiddy morning and seen me a sight. Biddy in the middle of that tiny piece of a living room waving her arms around like she some windup toy.

"Girl, this a new way of cleaning cobwebs?"

Biddy put on her sassy face and voice and say, "Lot you know. I'm doing tie chee." She flop her arms around more and look over her shoulder. "This is called Looking Back at the Moon."

I look over my shoulder. "You see a moon in here?"

Biddy make like she holding a big ball 'gainst her stomach. "Now I'm rolling the chee." She grinned at me real big. "At first I thought Miss Lizzy was talking about cheese, but it's just one chee."

I went to the kitchen.

"Girl, I think you done got the duck rabies for sure. I cain't tell if you're washin' 'em up or hangin' 'em out."

Biddy stop flopping and whirling and put one hand on her hip.

"This here is tie chee. It's Miss Lizzy's exercise for her dizzy ear. I watch her do it and she tell me about it. It's fun. I couldn't remember none of it until she tell me the name is kind of like what you do. Look, see, this is Monkey Holding Up the World."

Biddy push her arms up like she holding something heavy.

I shake my head. "This be Quincy Leaving the Loony Bin." I head for Lizabeth's.

When I walk into the kitchen, I found Lizabeth in a heap by the refrigerator. She was crying and pounding the floor with her fist.

"Lord, what happen? You hurt?"

"Just help me get up."

Lizabeth was crying, but crying mad, so I eased down some. I got holt of her under her arms, and she slid one arm over my shoulders.

"I know you don't like to be touched, Quincy, but . . ."

I didn't say nothing, I just got her over to the kitchen chair. Her walker was setting right there.

Lizabeth pull a handkerchief out her pocket. Wouldn't you know she wouldn't use no tissue? She dry her eyes and wipe her nose and then sigh real big. "Well, shit!"

I drop my butt into the other chair. My eyes must have goggled plumb out my head.

"Oh, don't look at me like that," she say. "I can cuss a blue streak if I damn well feel like it and I damn well feel like it!"

I shut my mouth and blinked, but I still couldn't do much else.

"Quincy, three years ago, I played tennis twice a week." Lizabeth wadded her handkerchief into her fist. "Sure, I was in a seniors' league, but I was on my own two feet." She smack the table with her fist. "Now I can't get from the table to the refrigerator without falling on my ass."

I wish I could pet her hand the way she does Biddy's when Biddy is all in a knot, but my hand won't reach out.

Lizabeth keep talking 'bout the doctors give her pills and sometime they help for a while, then they stop working. And her friends were good people, but they had their own busy lives and she couldn't do the things they did and they didn't come around so much anymore. How she was left all alone and on her ass.

I thought she was talking to me, and I felt my hand starting to unfreeze when she stare up at nothing, the way Biddy did when she said she was looking back at the moon, and said, "It's not like this misery is my fault."

Didn't she know who she was talking to? I thought she was talking to me like she understood how I felt to be left out. Like her and me was some alike. Alone and busted up. But then she say about fault and that tell she was only thinking about her ownself. She crazy if she think fault gots anything to do with it. Does she think misery only matter if you rich and smart and don't have no messed-up face?

I got up and started breakfast.

Biddy

Quincy's a hard one to figure. Miss Lizzy, she gets fretty, but she still the same Miss Lizzy. Just Miss Lizzy gone fretty. But Quincy ain't that way. Sometimes she's got that chicken-snake face. There's nothing Miss Lizzy or me can say or do that don't get us a mean look or a mean word. Other times, Quincy is easy-pleasy. Seem like when she mad at Miss Lizzy, Quincy get most nice to me. I can't figure that. And Miss Lizzy, she watch Quincy like it make her sad to see Quincy puff up and sulkish. Lately, I catch sight of Miss Lizzy watching me. I can't figure out why.

I wish people was as easy to understand as Mama Duck. Mostly, I try to clean what needs it. Talk to who-ever ain't in no bad mood. I know one thing. Even if Miss Lizzy and Quincy are hard to understand, I still feel smarter here. Ain't no other kids making fun. Ain't nobody giving me stuff I don't know how to do. I feel good here. If all I got to put up with is Quincy being sulkish, that's easy.

Quincy

Yesterday Lizabeth's friend came to get her. They went in her friend's big car for what she call "spa day." She was going to get her hair cut and have her nails done and then go play bridge with other ladies. She set it up on my day off from the Brown Cow and give Biddy and me tickets to the movie. She said it was a little treat for all the nice things we do for her. Biddy 'bout jump out her skin.

I figured out Biddy ain't never been to no movie show. Her granny need a good whoopin' for that. We gonna have to ride the bus and be with lots of people, so I tole her she could wear her coat.

Biddy wrapped up in her coat and didn't say nothing to nobody on the bus. When we get to the movie, we got us some popcorn and then we got us a surprise.

"Quincy, is that you? And Biddy?"

A girl wore a striped vest and stood next to a silver pole with a velvet rope hooked to it. She took people's tickets, tore off a piece, and then said, "Number one, that way," and pointed down the hall, or "That's in number seven, down that way," and pointed off the other direction.

That girl was Tasha Wells. She was a Speddie that graduated a year before Biddy and me.

Tasha took our tickets and pulled off a piece and handed them back. "You two gonna like this movie. It's real funny."

"You work here?" I axt.

"Sure do," she said. "Been working here since I graduated." She waved us to the side and took some people's tickets. "Number two," she said, and pointed.

"Good to see you, Quincy," Tasha said. "You too, Biddy."

I jerk Biddy along by her coat sleeve.

"Quincy?" Biddy say.

"What?"

"I never did think about other Speddies. Living in they own little places and having jobs just like us."

I didn't say nothing. Sure, other Speddies had jobs. But I never thought about 'em being Speddies we knew.

We found our movie and sat down. Biddy kept her head tuck down like she was still scared, until the movie got to going. It was a cartoon movie with cats and dogs that talk. Pretty soon, Biddy was giggling a little, down inside her ole coat, and then she was sitting up and laughing right out loud with the other folks.

That make me feel better than the popcorn.

Biddy

I wonder why I never thought about that. Other Speddies having jobs. She talked to me like I was a real person. She didn't call me a name. It was too much for me to get hold of when I was so scaredy already. Too much was happening to me in one day.

The movie was real funny, about cats that said funny things to dogs. The cats was smart and sassy like Quincy is. The dogs was sweet but kind of dumb. I had a real good time.

Quincy

Days still easing on by. But ever once in a while, Robert watch from his friend's car. Oncet they follow me home. I didn't look at them or say nothing.

Biddy kept watch on Mama Duck. Mama Duck kept watch on Biddy. She let Biddy give her corn and water, but hiss and peck when Biddy go to pet her. If that girl don't get the duck rabies, she's for sure gonna get duck lice.

Lizabeth stay worried and sad looking when she look at Biddy. Like when Biddy didn't know Lizabeth was watching her. This went for a good while. Then one morning when I went in early to cook breakfast, Lizabeth was sitting at the kitchen table holding a envelope.

"Quincy, I would like you to do me a favor."

I kept husht.

Lizabeth helt out her envelope. "Please mail this on your way to work." She sat for a minute, and I swear, that ole lady look like she was shamed.

"And, I'm sorry that I must ask you this, but don't tell Biddy anything about it. I know that this is a kind of lie, but it's nothing that will hurt her."

Lizabeth sigh. "I don't know how much Biddy can read or how much she knows."

I look down at the envelope. The Honorable and Mrs. Richard J. Barnes. I didn't know 'bout who Honorable was, but I knew the name. That was the judge in town. And I knew me a secret about that judge. Now my mind got in a knot. Did Lizabeth know that secret too? Did she know that I knowed? And why write the judge? And why can't Biddy know? Lord, I wisht I could get this tangle smoothed out.

I nod my head at Lizabeth and tuck the envelope in the big pocket of my uniform and tend to breakfast.

Biddy

Something not right at breakfast this morning. Quincy talking real fast. And trying to hurry me up. Like if I didn't get my eggs eat real fast, they was going to fly off the plate. I can't read too many words, but I can read a clock just fine. Quincy not late for work. I swear I can't ever get her figured out.

Quincy

Felt like that letter would burn a hole in my pocket, but I finally got breakfast over with and set off to the post office. I got to work a few minutes early and I saw me a sight in the break room. Jen was holding a pack of ice to Ellen's mouth. Jen kind of crunched her eyebrows together and shook her head, so I didn't say nothing. I closed the door and went on out to my work counter.

Biddy

Today, I done a stack of ironing. I ironed a bunch of tablecloths and napkins and even Miss Lizzy's pillowcases. She don't tell me to iron her pillowcases. I do it for a treat. So they all smooth under her face. I spray them with good-smelling water she keeps in her laundry room before I set the iron to them.

Miss Lizzy sat with me for a little while and talk. She talk about her little boy. About when he died. He had a disease that was a science name. She said it was a blood disease, about a luke. She talk about he was just a little boy. How sad it was. How much she miss him. That she just wish she could see him one time. Just to touch him.

I know how she felt. My baby ain't dead. But I can't touch her. I sure wish I could.

After Miss Lizzy told me her story, I come up here and tell mine into this tape. I'm making this a tape by its self. I maybe think my child wouldn't like to know this part. It's part of her remembery, but maybe it's cruel. Folks been cruel to me, and I don't want ever to be cruel to my child.

* * *

I was pretty once. That's not bragging on myself. It's a fact. People said I was pretty. And I was skinny. Until sixth grade. Then I started getting boobs and hips.

My clothes got tight in some places, and boys whistled and said, "You be fine!" And they try to rub up against me and laugh that . . . laugh. Not a happy laugh. One that scared me.

But I was dumb. I didn't know.

In seventh grade, things was going good and I was used to the whistles. The boys only talked and pushed against me. And the laugh didn't scare me so much.

Here's the part I don't like to say. I don't like to think it. But I got to tell the truth on this tape.

I . . . I sorta . . . liked boys talking to me. And wanting me to talk to them. Granny didn't talk to me 'cept to holler. I never had no friends. People called me White Trash and dumb and like that.

I thought those boys liked me.

Quincy

I made us a good dinner of pork chops that was grilled with special sauce and potatoes cut thin and sautéed in butter and fresh green beans.

I was full of confusion and upset and jangling pans and silverware, sounded like a whole circus show.

"Has something happened to get you in a tizzy, Quincy? You seem off-footed," Lizabeth said.

I decided to tell them. "I work with a woman name Ellen. She got a husband. Today she come in with her face all busted up. Jen tole me that Ellen's husband done it. He drinks. And when he gets all liquored up, he wants her paycheck so he can go drink some more. Ellen didn't want to give him her paycheck 'cause he drinks up all the rent money. So he bust her in the face and beat her up."

I stopped and looked at Biddy and Lizabeth. "Here's the thing. This ain't the first time he done it. He does this a lot."

Biddy and Lizabeth just sat there.

I stopped cutting my chop. "Cain't you two say boo to a ghost?"

Lizabeth made a little face I couldn't figure out. "What are we supposed to say?"

I couldn't believe my ears. "Lizabeth! This ain't no Special Ed girl. This is a full-growed-up woman. She don't have to let no man knock her around like that."

Lizabeth looked like she was gonna cry. "Quincy, do you think that you have to let someone treat you badly because you're Special Ed?"

I got all the over fidgets then. "No, that's not it. I . . ." Biddy was staring into her plate. She sure wasn't going to be no help.

"It's just Ellen and Jen is my friends and it don't seem right that they . . . I mean . . . Ellen, she's growed up—she should know better. . . ." I husht. That ole lady don't know what she's talkin' about.

"Just never mind about the whole thing," I said.

Biddy

I get up early to check Mama Duck. Around sunup, she flies off and leaves her eggs. I got scaredy the first morning. I ready to put a towel on her eggs to keep them warm, when Mama Duck come flying home. She lit in the yard. Waddled to her eggs. Set right down. She wiggled and waggled and squirmed. She used her beak to push her eggs around just right. Then she drank water.

I feel OK. She had to leave her babies to do her business. But she come right home to them.

Miss Lizzy's been poorly. I don't know why. 'Cause she don't want to talk. She whispered on the phone one morning. Then she acted a little better. Maybe a old lady sickness that passed.

I been scrubbing and putting a shine on that old house. It makes me smile to see how nice it looks when I get through with it.

I feel funny today. Like something missing and I don't 'zactly know what. It isn't like something that makes me sad to miss it. Then I know. It's been a while now. One whole calendar page since we moved here.

That means it's been one calendar page since somebody called me bad names. It's been that long since some boy said nasty things to me.

And now I got my own little house. A room with a princess table. Miss Lizzy and Mama Duck. And I got me a friend. Sometimes I don't know what to do with this much happy.

Quincy

This morning I thought the sky done fall. It was barely dawn o'clock when Biddy come squealing into my room.

"You got to see, Quincy!" That fool girl jerk the cover off me. I jump up ready to slap her sideways.

"It's a baby duck. We got a baby duck!"

I decide not to kill the silly girl right this minute. I'd go look at the duck first. "Biddy, don't come in here snatching covers off me. You gonna get hurt thataway. And you ain't got no baby duck. I didn't see you lay no egg."

But I was talking to her backside. Time I got down to the garden, Biddy on her knees peeking behind the bush. I swear I see more of that girl's hindparts than make me happy. I squat down and, sure 'nuff, there's a fuzzy baby duck just a-peeping around.

"Ain't she the cutest baby duck you ever saw?" Biddy say.

"It's the only baby duck I ever saw."

Biddy was off walking on clouds, and she babbled away. "Its name is Li'l Peep."

I shook my head. "You named this duck? Biddy, I swear they gonna lock you in a loony bin. . . ."

Biddy kept on a-chattering. "You the prettiest baby duck in the whole wide world. Your mama gonna take good care of you, and you gonna grow up to a fine duck."

She push her nose closer to the little duck, and Mama Duck snake out her neck and pop Biddy a good one. Mama Duck hiss and snort and cluck and quack up a blue streak. We back away and Mama Duck settle her feathers.

"They was a bunch of eggs. How come they's just one baby?" I axt.

"The rest will hatch out real quick. We gonna have us a whole herd of cute baby ducks," Biddy say whilst she rub her duck-bit nose.

"We gonna have us a whole pile of duck doo is what we gonna have," I say.

Biddy kept watching Mama Duck and Li'l Peep, but I got tired of squatting. I stood up. "I'm goin' back to sleep. I figure the rest of them ducks can hatch without me."

Biddy didn't pay me no mind. I'd have to sprout a few feathers to get her attention.

When I woke back up, Lizabeth was outside in her walker watching Biddy watch the duck.

"Well, Quincy, what do you think about the new addition to our family?"

I rock back on my heels and stare Lizabeth down. "Last time I checked, nobody in my fambly had a beak or web feets." I stood up and push past her. "Or white hair and wrinkles, neither." I couldn't stop my mouth. "Nobody in my fambly fat and blondey, neither, so don't be pushin' you ownselfs into my fambly."

I look at Lizabeth feelin' kinda proud of standin' up for my ownself and saw that old lady look like I done crush her face with a rock. I know how that feel. Then her face change.

Biddy

I couldn't believe my two ears. Leave it to Quincy to spoil things. Miss Lizzy did something I ain't never seen her do. She got mad.

She turned to Quincy. She grabbed the sides of her walker until her knuckles stood out. Her voice wasn't loud. No hollering or screaming from Miss Lizzy. She looked sad. But I could see her black eyes was hard and snappy.

She told Quincy that she tried hard to understand that peoples been mean to her and that Quincy always 'spected the worst out of folks. But she said manners meant more than holding a spoon right. She said that Quincy couldn't treat peoples bad just 'cause she wanted to.

Miss Lizzy took a deep breath. And kind of run out of steam. But she said me and her been kind to Quincy, and she was disappointed in her.

Miss Lizzy thumped her walker and stamped past Quincy. Quincy stood there.

Miss Lizzy got to the door. She turned around. "And don't step foot in my kitchen until you are ready to be courteous to me . . . and to Biddy."

She went inside.

I saw something then I didn't know what to do with.

Quincy started crying.

She didn't cry like most peoples. Her eyes got full-up with tears that got bigger than Quincy could handle. Then they run down her face. She didn't do nothing to stop it. She stood there, her back straight and her head up. Tears run down her cheeks, over her chin, and down her neck and shirt collar.

I didn't know how to feel. I was full-up with proud that Miss Lizzy told Quincy to treat me right. I felt sorry for Quincy too. I know what it was like to have people talk bad to you. Make you cry. But I was mad at Quincy. She spoiled the whole morning. My baby duck morning. I wanted to push her in the dirt. Stomp on her back. And . . . and I wanted to pat her on her back. Tell her not to cry.

I cleared my throat.

Quincy put her hand up like Ms. Evans when she wanted hush in class.

I 'spected Quincy to run up the steps to our house and start packing. But she done something made my brain twirl.

She lifted up the hem of her T-shirt and wiped her face. Then she turn around. She took a deep breath. She looked me square in my eye.

"Biddy, I'm sorry I'm such a shit."

Then she marched herself into Miss Lizzy's house. Pretty soon I heard cabinet doors closing and pans clanking. I sat down on the grass. I didn't know what to do or where to go.

In a little while I smelled cinnamon. I knew Quincy was making her Yummy French Toast.

She called to Miss Lizzy to come eat breakfast.

Quincy was sorry. I didn't think that girl could be sorry for nothing. Sometimes you gotta wait a long time to find what's true.

Quincy

I was bad mean to Lizabeth and Biddy, and Lizabeth, she set me straight. It wasn't so much she hopping mad, but more like she tired to the bone of my hateful self. I did my 'pologizin' and made breakfast. Once the kitchen smelled of cinnamon and butter, I easied down.

I scrub myself hard in the shower, wishing that mean part of me could wash away under hot water. But I know it be deeper down.

I don't get Lizabeth. Once I say I was sorry, she smile nice. Not fake. And she pet my hand. And I didn't flinch or jerk it back. It was like nothing been crostways between us. I don't know how to let go a grudge. It's like it grows onto my body and get to be a new part of me.

Maybe when you live rich and with smart in your head, your hurts don't get so sore.

Biddy

It's been two days. None of the other eggs have hatched. Mama Duck still sitting on them, though. And, Li'l Peep swimming around in that pan of water. And, they're both eating the dry corns. But I'm worried.

Quincy

I come home, and Biddy sitting next to that pile of eggs. She tuck a little blanket on them. Mama Duck and Li'l Peep was nowhere around. Biddy be crying. Not one of her snot-nose sobbing jags, but crying like her heart done broke.

I left her alone and went and found Stephen where he was pulling weeds in the front yard.

"Are them eggs gonna ever hatch?"

"No," he said.

Two days later, when Biddy asleep, I went outside and buried them eggs.

Biddy never said a word about it.

Biddy

I walked to the feed store to talk to the clerk man. I told him about the eggs. He said that the mama left them because they was probly " 'fective." I didn't know what that meant. He told me that there was something wrong with them.

Quincy

I got my money and went to the big Kmart. I bought Biddy a TV. It's little, but maybe some cartoons make her laugh. I'm so tired of that long face. I'd be glad to hear her sing 'bout the Itsy-Bitsy Spider.

Biddy

I wonder if my child knows she's 'dopted. I decided that I'm not going to give her these tapes. If she don't know she's 'dopted, she won't never feel like her mama left her.

Quincy

Things ain't been right around home. My head is addled 'bout Biddy and Lizabeth. Lizabeth been acting funny. Like she got a surprise in the back room. I got me a bad feeling.

Biddy

It's late. Gone dark. Quincy not home. Miss Lizzy worried too. But she said, "Have patience, Biddy." She told me Quincy eighteen and free to do like she please, and it wasn't real late. She said that if Quincy wasn't home by ten, she'd make some calls.

I know Quincy wasn't out having fun. She belonged home. I don't want to go on them dark streets. I'm scaredy of it. Maybe boys being around. But Quincy needs me.

I got my coat and pulled it close. It's big on me now, like all my clothes. I left out of the house and walked to the Brown Cow.

I didn't look at nobody. I put one foot in front of the other one and kept on. When I got to the Brown Cow, I went to the side where ready-made food was.

"Is Quincy here?" I asked the worker lady.

The woman's eyebrows went up. "She left at six. That's when she gets off."

I know time. I looked at the big clock over the lady's head. It said almost nine o'clock. My stomach hurt. I wished I could clean something. Quincy would come home and everything would be OK.

I left and walked down the alley behind the store. Maybe Quincy walks home this way. I went down that alley a ways. It led to another alley. That's when I heard it.

It was a little sound. I stopped walking. I tilted my head this side and that so I could find it. I heard it again. A "mew" sound, but kind of, I don't know, maybe a hurt kitten. I went down a side alley. I couldn't hear the sound no more. I went back to the alley from before. I seen something. A tennis shoe sticking out between two Dumpsters. There was leg attached to the shoe. I run up and saw the worst thing I ever did see.

Quincy was curled up in a ball. Her bottom half was naked. Her uniform pants tied over her head. Her shirt was pushed up. Her stomach and chest was bleeding. Quincy stayed curled up tight, that one foot sticking out. Her fingers scratched in and out of the alley dirt. And she mewed inside that sack.

I knew how she felt.

I knew.

I knew what to do. I couldn't go screamy. I had to stay easy. I had to help my friend.

I stepped closer but didn't touch her. "Quincy?"

Quincy give a gaspy sound. Pulled her hands 'cross her stomach.

"Quincy, it's Biddy. I'm gonna help you."

Quincy got real still. She put her hand out. "Get away from me."

I kneeled down. I didn't touch. "No, not gonna do it. You need me to help. You're bleeding on your stomach, and . . . other places."

Quincy mewed again. I never heard such a sad sound. I guess I made that sound before. It hurt me to hear Quincy make it.

"I'm gonna untie these pants legs on top your head. You put your hands right here 'gainst mine so you know that's what I'm doing. I ain't gonna hurt you."

Quincy reached up and grab hold of my wrists. Her pants was tied in a doubled-up knot. It took me a while in that shadowy alley to get it figured out. I pulled them over her head. Quincy let loose of my wrists. She put her hands over her face, hiding it.

I done that too.

"How bad is your stomach?" I asked.

"It's like deep scratches. They didn't stab me." Quincy stopped, then made another mew sound. "Not with no knife."

"I know, Quincy. I know."

We didn't say no more. Then I came to myself. Remembered we was in a dark alley. Quincy mostly naked. "Let me help get your pants on and go home."

Quincy

I don't know how we got home. I kept my head down and my hands over my stomach. I didn't want nobody to see what was there. In the 'partment Biddy push me down on the couch.

"I don't know what to do," I tole her.

"I do," Biddy say.

I look at her. I 'spect she might have one of them faces like a cat that done ate a bird. Her knowing that I'm just like her now.

But she look like she did when she looked at those cold duck eggs Mama Duck left behind.

"Do we gotta tell Lizabeth?" I axt.

Biddy shook her head. Sad-like. "Better not. Nice as Miss Lizzy is, peoples change when they hear 'bout this kind of evil doing." She shook her head again. "All of a sudden you're dirty and they don't want to get it on them."

I thought I'd gotten holt of myself, but I blubbered again.

"I'm gonna put you in the shower. You wash till you feel clean. Run the water hot and use lots of soap."

Biddy lean into my face and made me look in her eyes. "I don't think you're dirty, but I know you feel like it. You wash till you feel some better. I'll make coffee. You gonna drink it, and I'm gonna tell you what to do next."

Biddy

I made instant coffee. Sat on a stool at our counter table. Quincy took a long shower. I think she didn't stop until the hot water run out. She came out wrapped up in her thick robe. She sat. Her hands was shaking so bad, the coffee slopped. She didn't look at me.

"You got to tell me about it. If you don't, you won't never be able to think of nothing else."

"I cain't," Quincy said.

"You got to."

She shook her head. She still didn't look at me.

"I'll tell you how it happened to me. I'll tell first. Would that make it OK?"

"I cain't look at you and tell you what they done."

An idea jumped in my head. I jumped up right after it.

"I can fix this."

Quincy

Biddy jump off her stool and run to her room. She come back quicker than a lizard's lick. She slap a tape on the counter right in front of me.

"Go in your room. Tell on this tape. And I'll go tell on mine. Then we trade."

"Biddy, this ain't gonna make it go away." I open my bathrobe so Biddy could see HO cut into my chest and stomach. Not deep enough to kill me, just deep enough to make scars.

"That say 'Ho,' " I tell her.

Biddy's white face turnt plumb ghosty. "It ain't true," she say. "You don't never go thinking it's true."

I wrap my robe around and pick up her tape. Telling what happen or hearing her story wouldn't make nothing be different. But if Biddy say I wasn't no ho, I'd do anything she axt.

Biddy

A boy named Dale come up when I walked out of school. He said I was the prettiest girl he ever seen. That I was sweet as candy. I smiled. Said I liked candy.

He told me he had lots of candy in his daddy's barn. He'd give me some. Maybe I'd give him a kiss.

I wanted candy. Kissing him might not be bad. He stepped close. Picked up a piece of my hair. Rubbed it. He smelled of it. "Smells sweet, like flowers," he said.

I wanted him to kiss me then. I thought he liked me. I wanted somebody to say nice things to me. Not call me Retard.

I went with him.

I walked in his daddy's barn. He shut the door. Put a board across to lock it.

Boys came out of the shadowy part of the barn. The dark parts. Where I couldn't see. They come rushing at me out of the dark. They grabbed me. Pushed me down on the hay. One held my arms. Another one held my legs. They pulled my shirt up. My pants down. They took off my underwear. Pushed it in my mouth.

And they done it to me. Every one of 'em. Dale done it twice. They done other stuff too.

Once they was done, they zipped up their pants. They laughed. They slapped each other's hands high in the air, then low. Laughed some more.

Dale looked down at me while I tried to cover myself and said, "Want some candy, Ho? I'll give you more candy anytime you want it."

Then he spit on me.

Then the other boys spit on me.

Quincy

I finish work and put my apron in the bin that go out to the laundry. I was fidgety 'bout some stuff and wasn't careful. I walk through the parking lot like usual, and somebody jump out from between the cars. Robert. He run through the cars and grab holt of me before my head tole my feet to run. He clapt his hand on my mouth and his arm 'round my waist and dragged me. His friend jump out his car and grab holt of my feet. They threw me in and Robert sat on my head so I couldn't holler.

Robert said, "Get goin', Darrel." The car went fast and Robert got off my head, but he put a knife to my face. "I can't make you no uglier, but I can cut your tongue out and I can gut you like a fish. You want me to do that, Ho?"

I shut my eyes and shake my head. I couldn't do nothin' but leak tears. Nothin' else in my whole body worked.

Darrel stopped the car. Robert say, "Darrel, I don't know. She be too ugly to get me a stiffy."

"You got to get them pants off her ugly butt anyways, so put 'em over her head," Darrel say.

Robert look at me. "That might work. Her butt bound to look better than her face." Darrel got out the car and come 'round the side. Robert open the door and both of them jerk my pants off, pull them over my head, and tied 'em tight.

I felt the ripped-up places of the car seat sticking my bare skin. Robert got on me. He say, "You deserve this, bitch. No ho gonna dis me." He shove in hard. It hurt me bad. He kept doing it, and he cuss in my ear the whole time. Calling me names.

When he was done, he tole Darrel to take his turn. So Darrel did. He didn't say nothing to me. I could hear Robert laugh.

Then Robert shove my shirt up. He say, "This is so you remember what you is, skank." He cut me.

They got in the front seat and drove. They stop and dump me out. Robert say if I tole anybody, he'd kill me. Darrel say they friends would help kill me. They say the police won't care 'bout no ugly ho. But they'd kill me anyway. Just because they could.

Biddy

After we listened to each other's tapes, I went to Quincy's room. I sat on her bed. "You know they're right, don't you?"

"Which part? Me being a ho or the part that they can kill me?"

"I told you before you ain't no ho. You got to believe it in your own head."

"I keep thinking I must of done sumpin' made them think . . ."

I didn't let her finish. Quincy always talks real loud when she wants a body to understand. So I raised up my voice. Kind of hollered right in her face. "If you cook me dinner—and I don't want to eat it—and you shove the food down my throat, then who's the bad one? Me or you?"

Quincy close her eyes and tears leak out. She wipe her cheek with the sash of her robe. Then she laughed. I thought she gone crazy.

"How'd you get so smart? You cain't even read."

I stared. Trying to figure out what was what. Maybe I needed to put her back in the shower. With cold water this time.

Quincy nodded her head. "We gonna call the police and get that piece of trash arrested."

Quincy looked so happy. I hated to make her sad again. But I had to. "Quincy, you're right. But other peoples won't believe it. Police or nobody else care what happen to girls like us."

All the air seemed to go out of her. None of that Quincy-fight no more.

"You right," she said real quiet.

"You can't tell nobody." I handed her another tape. "This will tell you why."

Quincy

I'm all mixed up. I feel one way, then I feel another, and then I don't know what I feel or what to think or how to do. If it wasn't for Biddy, I'd fly off into pieces. I took Biddy's new tape and put it in the player. She stayed right beside me while I listened.

Biddy

I got dressed. I threw my underwear in a ditch when I left the barn.

When I got home, I told Granny what those boys done. She slapped me 'cross my face and called me Slut. Said I was no good like my mama. Told me I got what I deserved and to quit sniveling.

She wouldn't let me take a bath. Told me to sleep with the smell of rut so I'd learn to keep my legs together.

I got all the candy and cookies in the house and pinned them inside my coat. So nobody could trick me again.

I never told what happened. I know those boys told that I ask them to do me. I know telling my story wouldn't make peoples change they minds.

I never know when my monthlies was gonna come around, but I started puking in the morning sometime later. Granny told me I was pregnant.

I wore my coat and Granny bought me big T-shirts. I ate everything I could.

When I had my baby, Granny and the doctor told me to print my name on a piece of paper. They said it was the baby's birth 'tificate. I signed it like they said.

Later, Granny told me that the paper said that I gave my baby away. And I couldn't do nothing about it. She said if I tried to get my baby back, I'd go to jail, because the baby's new parents paid my hospital. It would be like I was stealing.

That scared me real bad. Granny told me I was too stupid to raise a child. She told me that my child was a normal child. Shouldn't be stuck with such as me. I guess that true. I miss my baby. I would like to have held it. Sung it to sleep.

Quincy

I don't like touching nobody, but I put my hand on Biddy's like Lizabeth do. It was almost like her pain made mine easy down. But I felt bad too. I knew for sure that I couldn't tell 'bout Robert. I'd pay more for telling than I'd ever get back. And if I tole on Robert and he did come to find me and kill me, he'd as like hurt Biddy too. Biddy been hurt enough for stuff that wasn't ever her fault.

I needed me another shower.

Biddy

I never listened to my tapes before. I felt strange hearing my voice. It made me sadder listening to how Granny done me than when it happened. I wonder why. Quincy pat my hand. Took another shower. I figured she'd be taking lots of showers now. It's hard to feel clean again. You have to scrub everything around you to feel even a little better.

I found some ointment. Quincy found a box that she said was First Aid. We learned about that in our classes. I knew there would be bandages. Quincy let me put ointment on her stomach cuts. I covered them with a white bandage. I think she felt better with that word covered.

I told Quincy to go to bed. I'd sleep on the floor in her room. I was used to sleeping on a pallet. It surprised me when Quincy didn't argue.

I don't think Quincy slept. She tossed in bed. I heard her crying. I didn't know nothing else to do but be there.

Next morning, Quincy took another shower. After I made her a new bandage, I trotted her Brown Cow uniform to Miss Lizzy washer. I told Miss Lizzy that Quincy had flu. Could she call the Brown Cow and tell them? I made Miss Lizzy cereal and tea.

Quincy looked bad awful. Her eyes was swollen. Her face had bruises I hadn't seen last night. All her sass was gone.

"Quincy," I said, "this is the baddest thing that's ever gonna happen to you. There's gonna be nothing but good stuff now."

"Biddy, for people like us, they's nothing but a string of bad waiting."

I grabbed her and I hugged her tight.

Quincy

Biddy grab me in a hug. I stiff up to pull back, but Biddy wouldn't let go. She hug harder and pet the back of my head. Then the warm of it kind of seep in, and I sigh and let her hug. I bawled again. It be a different crying. The kind that feel good.

Biddy

Quincy slept the rest of the day. I fixed canned soup for supper. She ate it. She didn't talk, but she didn't seem so — I don't know — I don't got a word for it. We sat in front of our TV. Watched some shows.

The next day and the day after, I told Miss Lizzy that Quincy was still poorly. Then it was Quincy's regular day off. She got up late that morning. We ate cereal for lunch.

"What Lizabeth been eating?" she asked.

Quincy hadn't said nothing for so long that I almost caught me hiccups from the surprise.

"I been warming soup. I made salad."

"I guess she ain't dead yet. You cain't do much harm with that stuff."

It was good for Quincy to fuss.

Quincy look me up and down. She reached out and give me a fast hug. She backed up like she scare herself.

"I'm getting dressed. This bathrobe is funky smelling. Besides, we got us something to do."

"What?" I asked Quincy.

"I'm teaching you to cook."

Quincy

Biddy got all scared in her face.

"Lord, girl, I said I was teaching you to cook—I ain't gonna cook you."

"I'm too stupid to learn cooking."

I rubbed my nose a minute so I could think. I put my face on up into Biddy's. "If I ain't dirty, you ain't stupid."

I watched Biddy whilst she pondered. She chew her lip, tilt her head, and then bust out with one of her Biddy smiles. "I know what you saying, but I still cain't read."

I dust my hands against each other and push the sleeves of my robe up. "Don't got to. I'm gonna take care of that."

Biddy start to say something, but I kept talking. "Whilst I get out this robe, you go down to the garden. It's the last of vegetables, so we gonna use 'em for somethin' extra fine. Get us a big ole eggplant, and tomatoes, and a couple of them squashes."

Biddy went off happy to be doing something besides watching me mope.

I change into some clothes and come back out to see Biddy near about to wring her hand plumb off her wrists. There was no vegetables nowheres and Biddy looked ghostie white. All I could think was she done seen Robert out that door.

"You seen him, didn't you?" My voice went up high and scared, but I was mad too. Robert didn't have no truck comin' here and scarin' Biddy.

Biddy nod. "He's out there pullin' weeds in the vegetable garden."

Robert was pullin' weeds? Sumpin' wrong here. Robert not goin' pull no weeds. And how would Biddy know what Robert look like, come to think of it.

"Who pullin' weeds, Biddy?" I axted.

"That Stephen boy. Who else? I can't go down there and get"—she look up in the air and then count on her fingers—"a big eggplant, tomatoes, and a couple of squashes if he out there."

I went and look out the window. There he was, weeding away. I turned to Biddy. "We just have to wait till he leave for our vegetables."

It wasn't two minutes later we hear footsteps trompin' up our stairs and then a knock at our door—"Delivery for Biddy and Quincy"—and then footsteps back down the stair. I look out the window in a few minutes and I see Stephen squatting back down to weed.

I go open the door a crack and there set a big ole

eggplant, a batch of tomatoes, and four squashes. That boy done heard everything we said out the window. I open the door wider to pick up the vegetables, and Stephen, he stood up and said, "You be needing anything else, Quincy?"

I wanted to run back in our little apartment and hide, but something clomp me upside the head. This boy wadn't nothing like that Robert. He wadn't goin' hurt me. None at all.

"I could use onion, parsley, and green beans." Stephen nod and I shut the door. Pretty soon, he come a trompin' again, and then he knock. This time he didn't tromp away. I open the door, but Biddy be hidin' in her bedroom listenin' at the door like a scaredy child.

"Quincy," Stephen say, "I don't know what I might have done to scare Biddy so bad or make you so mad at me, but whatever it might be, I'm sure sorry. Miss Elizabeth says it's not my fault, but Biddy shakes and goes white if she sees me, and you look at me like your fists are in the air ready to swing at me, so I kind of think she's wrong about that. If we can't be friends, I wish for Miss Elizabeth's sake that we could be friendly to each other." He scratched his nose. "I wouldn't hurt neither of you two for the whole world. I know you are special to Miss Elizabeth and that's enough for me."

He scratch his nose again. "Boy, howdy, that's a lot of talk out of me at one time. I usually just do my job and don't talk much." He tried on a little ole grin. "So, can we try to get along a little bit for Miss Elizabeth's sake?" He hold out the vegetables.

And I got another clomp upside my head. I knew if I look in the mirror, I wouldn't see the same ole Quincy that I seen all the other days of my life.

I took the vegetables and say, "Thank you, Stephen. Biddy might still be scaredy of you for a while, but I promise I'll be friendly to you. You didn't do nothing wrong."

"Thank you. You enjoy those vegetables." He clomped on down the stairs and went back to his weedin'.

Now I knew why Biddy and me was put to be roommates. It wasn't because we graduated at the same time. Nobody else would have me but Biddy. Because I'm so mean. I fuss about people being bad to me, but I'm the one that always gots her fists up being not nice to peoples first. I'm the mean one. Always have been. Got hit with a brick and been hittin' other peoples back ever since. People that didn't do nothin' to me.

Then I shook my head. But Robert did something bad to me and I didn't do nothing wrong to him. I sassed him a little when he called me ugly, but that don't give him no call to . . . hurt me.

But Stephen didn't hurt me. And I don't think he'd hurt me nor Biddy neither. It's hard not to blame him and make him pay for what Robert did just 'cause Robert ain't here. Life is hard and muddled.

I got to cook me something and get my head a little straighter.

I got potatoes, carrots, garlic, and olive oil, put a knife on the counter, and set myself on the stool. "We gonna make us some ratatouille."

"Rat a what?" Biddy come out her bedroom lookin' a mite uneasy.

"That's a big word mean vegetable stew."

"Ain't no rats gonna be in this stew. I like all you cook, but, Quincy, I ain't eating no rats."

I felt myself 'bout to yell at that fool, when I see Biddy's mouth twitch. She was funning with me.

"I swear, Quincy. You cain't call nothing by a right name. This here you call an eggplant. It don't look like no egg, and I bet if you planted it, it wouldn't grow no baby eggs."

I shake my head at the girl, but I was feeling a chuckle somewheres.

"And you calls chocolate pudding 'moose.' I tell you, when I saw what was in that bowl, I was scaredy of what part of that moose we was eating."

Girl be trying to make me laugh.

"Now you got me making rat stew, and I'm chopping squash, not little whiskers and feets and tails."

I bust loose then. Nothing she said was all that

funny, but her trying hard to make me forget my troubles felt fine.

"Hush up, girlfriend, and wash them veggies. You gonna do all the cooking. I'm gonna sit up here like some kinda queen and give orders."

"If you the queen, then I'm a princess, so that's OK with me," Biddy say.

That same night, I start work on my secret project.

Biddy

Quincy showed me how to chop. I learned to put the point of the knife down. Use the back to cut. I was a little scaredy that I'd find one of my fingers in with the carrots. But I done it right.

When the vegetables was all cut up, Quincy told me how to put the stew together with herb-weeds and water. Set it to cook real slow. After a while, it started to smell real good.

It "simmered"—that's a Quincy word for slow cooking. Then I toss up a salad.

"I think we ought to eat first. See if one of us falls out dead before we take any to Miss Lizzy," I said.

"It be perfect."

So I gathered the stuff. I trotted it over to Miss Lizzy.

I told her that Quincy feeling some better. But not ready to spread her germs around.

Miss Lizzy looked sad and said, "I hope she gets better soon. I certainly miss your company."

I wished I could tell Miss Lizzy about what happened to Quincy. I was afraid. I didn't want to lose Miss Lizzy's good thoughts about us.

Back to our house, Quincy put place mats on the counter. Dished up the stew. I sat like a princess. I dipped my spoon. Lifted it to my lips and tasted.

It was good. It was a lots good. My head couldn't hardly believe what my tongue told it.

Quincy smiled. "You see anybody here too stupid to cook?"

Quincy

There was nothing for it but to go to work Monday. The cuts was scabbing over and the bruises lighter. I didn't sleep much, and when I did, I dreamed evil. I'd cry and have to get a cold washrag to lay over my eyes so they wouldn't get swole up.

I got up before the 'larm and made omelets at Lizabeth's. She smile and pet my hand and say she glad to see that I was recovered. I tried to smile, but it came out sideways. I drank my orange juice and coffee, but I couldn't do nothing with them eggs but stir 'em 'round my plate.

Biddy was plumb full of chat and tole Lizabeth 'bout how she learning to cook.

I got my plate away from the table without Lizabeth noticing that I didn't eat.

I went up to our apartment, brush my teeths, and put on my uniform. Biddy done washed and ironed 'em. I cried again when I pulled them pants on, but I fuss at myself hard and stop blubbering.

Biddy stood on the porch in her big coat.

"How come you ain't doing the dishes?"

"I'll do them when I get back," she say.

"From where?"

"I'm walking you to work," Biddy say.

"You don't like to go out in the world. And I ain't no little child. I can walk by myself."

"I feel like having a morning walk. Can't you nor nobody tell me I can't."

I sigh like I was mad at her, but the ache in the back of my head easied off.

Biddy walk along with me, chatting away like a chipmunk.

I don't know what she was saying 'cause I look for Robert and that ole car. It seem like we walk to Mars before we finally got to the Brown Cow. Biddy march me right up to the door and didn't leave till I went inside.

Biddy

I tried not to show how scaredy I was. I wanted to leave my coat in the closet. But that boy Robert might be out there. I couldn't let Quincy go alone, but I couldn't go without my coat.

I talked a blue streak to keep from turning tail and running back to our safe house. I saw Quincy slitting her eyes all around. She was looking for the same thing I was. Peoples with meanness.

I watched her go in the store. I walked fast and hard back to our home. I hung up my coat. I looked at it for a long time. I felt some ashamed. If Quincy had the gumption to go to work, why was I so scaredy that I had to wear my coat? I closed the closet door. I wasn't gonna wear it no more.

At Miss Lizzy's I dusted every knickknack in that big house. I scrubbed the kitchen floor, even though it was shiny.

Miss Lizzy must have been happy to see Quincy over her flu. She smiled and sang little bits of songs all the day. Just before Quincy was supposed to come home, the doorbell rang. I answered it and a man stood there with two flat boxes. "Delivery from Redmond's," he said.

Miss Lizzy thumped up behind me in her walker. "I'll take care of this, Biddy." I figured somebody done sent her a present.

"I'm gonna go for a walk, if that's OK," I told Miss Lizzy.

She nodded, busy signing for the deliveryman.

I walked to the Brown Cow without my coat and didn't get shiverish but once.

Quincy

Jen and Ellen axted how I was feeling. I tole them I was still tired as whupped pup. I wore a cloth mask over my nose and mouth. Tole 'em I didn't want to spread no germs. So I got left pretty much to my ownself.

I couldn't help but look for Robert. I was 'fraid he would jump out from behind the stacks of Cheerios and drag me outside.

It was a long ole day. I knew it would be a long day every day. I'd always be watching for Robert over my shoulder. I chopped and diced and minced, and then a thought started up in my head. It was hard for me to figure. It was like I had holt of the end of a string that was in a big tangly knot. If I pulled here, it got too tight there and the knot got worser. I worried at that knot all day, and finally the knot came undone all at oncet. As long as I kept my mouth shut, Robert didn't care nothing 'bout me. I didn't have to worry 'bout him no more. I was trash that he had throwed away.

When I got done with work, I dawdled putting my apron in the laundry. I took a long time picking out a just-right loaf of bread. I didn't want to walk out into that parking lot. Finally, I took me a deep breath and head out.

And there was Biddy. I never thought I'd ever feel happy to see that fool girl.

"Where's your coat?" I axt her.

"Hi, Biddy. It's good to see you," she say to me.

I stop and look at her hard so she wouldn't know that I was bumfoozled. Why that girl saying hello to herself? Then I got it. She was funning with me again, but she was trying to teach me a lesson too. Like Lizabeth done her about table manners.

"Hi, Biddy. Good to see you," I say. "Now, where's your coat?"

"Not cold enough for a coat," Biddy say.

"Never was."

That cold, hard feeling I always had inside me felt like it be slipping a bit sideways. Biddy is plumb scared to come out in the world, and she was coming here to protect me from Robert.

Tears run down my face. I had me too many jumble-up feelings.

Biddy

I done laundry while Quincy cooked up something. I helped set the table and called Miss Lizzy.

"This is good, Quincy. What you call it?" I asked.

"This be Chicken Parmesan à la Quincy."

I felt my face go stupid. I figured Quincy would make fun of me. But she smiled.

"That means it's chicken that has a kind of red sauce and cheese on it. The 'à la Quincy' is saying made by Quincy."

I smiled. "I believe you the best cook in the world."

"I'll teach you how to make it," Quincy said.

Miss Lizzy look up and Quincy remind her she teaching me to cook.

"That's lovely," Miss Lizzy said. "And what will Biddy teach you in return, Quincy?"

I wasn't smart enough to teach. I felt bad.

Quincy looked straight in my face. "Biddy already teaching me lots. Mostly how to be nice to folks that never hurt me."

My chest 'bout bust open.

We talked and finished our dinner. Miss Lizzy stayed at her chair while I took the dishes. She put her hand on Quincy's so she couldn't get up. Quincy jumped when Miss Lizzy touched her. Pulled her hand back. When Miss Lizzy look hurt, Quincy got all upset in her face. "I don't want you to get no germs," she said.

"That's considerate of you, Quincy." She clear her throat like she got a hair ball in it. "I have something important to talk to the two of you about," Miss Lizzy said. "I have a special visitor coming here tomorrow evening. Quincy, would you go into the living room? There are two boxes on the sofa and I'd like you to bring them in here."

Quincy toted those two boxes I seen the deliveryman bring.

"These are for you, girls. The top one is for Biddy and the other is yours, Quincy." Miss Lizzy waved her hand. "Open them, please."

Quincy and me took our boxes. Opened the lids. There was softy pink paper and—a dress. Quincy had a dress too.

Something felt wrong. My teachers give me a dress for graduation. This felt—different. I know without looking at Quincy there was thunder and lightning about to bust out. Maybe I helped Quincy learn about how to be nice to peoples that hadn't hurt us—but Miss Lizzy just hurt us plenty. Only I didn't know the how or the why of it.

Quincy

Biddy and I helt up those dresses and then look 'crosst at one 'nother. Lizabeth watch us like she 'spect us to fall on the floor and kiss her bony feet.

I drop the dress back in the box and dust off my hands like they was dirty. Biddy lay hers back in the box and put the lid on real careful.

Lizabeth look from Biddy to me and back again. "Don't you like them?"

Nobody said nothing.

"Wouldn't you try them on? I'd like to see how you look."

We still didn't say nothing. All that nothing was makin' a big noise. And all the good dinner smell turn sour.

"I don't understand," Lizabeth say.

Biddy look at Lizabeth and nod her head.

I been trying to hold back my bad mouth, but when I saw that beat-up look on Biddy's face, I couldn't help myself.

"Lizabeth, I don't got the right words, but this is like telling us we're stupid."

Biddy had her face all twisted up like she was puzzling something out, but when I said that, she seem like she understood what was wrong now.

But Lizabeth didn't.

"What? I gave you a present."

Biddy's voice sound like she was talking through a stack of pillows. "No, Miss Lizzy. This ain't no present."

Lizabeth got mad. "I know your teacher gave you a dress for graduation. You weren't so particular then."

Biddy looked like she been hit in her stomach.

My mad boil right over.

"Don't you talk to Biddy like that. You want to be mean about Biddy not havin' a graduation dress—you go be mean to her granny. And Biddy's teacher let her pick out her graduation dress. She didn't say, 'Here, dress up like I think you should.'"

Biddy wiped tears off her face. She used her fists and knuckles like a little child. That hurt me inside my heart some kind of way.

Lizabeth folded the paper back over one of the dresses. She looked a little shamed but she still had some mad in her.

"I don't see that—"

"Biddy and me earn money now. We bought our own clothes. But you think we're too stupid to dress proper for your friend. You didn't give us these dresses for us. You bought them for you. To make sure when you trot us out we don't embarrass you. Like we was your pet dogs."

"Quincy! I've told you before that you must keep a civil tongue—"

"Lizabeth, Biddy and me ain't your pets. We ain't your good deed. You done been mean to Biddy and me and I'm telling you about it. Now you been told."

Lizabeth turnt to Biddy. "Biddy, surely you don't . . ."

"Quincy's right. This ain't a present."

"Fine, if you feel that way, I'll send the dresses back." Lizabeth pull herself up and into her walker. "Please be in your 'good dresses' tomorrow evening to meet my guest."

"You still don't get it, do you, Lizabeth?" I say.

"What now? If you don't want the dresses, fine. I told you that."

"You don't get to tell us. If we don't want the dresses, we don't need you to tell us it's OK. And we get paid to cook and clean. You cain't tell your retarded girls to parade out and show what a good woman you are."

Lizabeth gasped and Biddy dropped the glass she was holding.

That pretty glass broke all into pieces.

Biddy

I looked from the glass pieces on the floor. I saw tears in Miss Lizzy's eyes. It give me a start to know I was crying too. Then I looked over at Quincy. Tears was running down her face.

"I thought you two liked me," Miss Lizzy said real quiet.

"We thought you liked us," I said.

Miss Lizzy pushed out the kitchen. Quincy run past me out the back door. I picked up the sharp glass.

The next morning, Quincy fixed breakfast like always. Everybody sat on the edge of they chairs with straight backs. But we wasn't sitting like princesses.

Miss Lizzy ate her fruit. She sipped her tea. Then, without looking at me, she asked would I please meet her friend tonight.

"Yes, ma'am. You made all the plans."

"Quincy, would you mind serving the tea and dessert? It's important that Biddy talk to my visitor, and I can't handle the cups and plates."

Quincy nodded her head about half a nod.

"I'll pay you extra, of course, for your time."

I 'spected Quincy to blow up like a big bomb, but instead she got that hurt-to-the-bone look.

"Lordy, and folks think me and Biddy the ones that be 'challenged.'" She put her fork down on the edge of her plate. She stood up. "I'll be here. Keep your money."

She laid her napkin folded up nice on the table and left.

Miss Lizzy sighed. "Why can't I say anything right to that girl? I'm tired of fighting with her, worrying about every word I say."

I waited, thinking out my words. Letting Miss Lizzy settle a little.

"Miss Lizzy," I said. "If Quincy and me wasn't here and you invited some friends over for tea . . ." I had to stop. Get everything straight inside my head. "And you couldn't handle the teacups. Would you ask one of your friends to serve the cake?"

"Well, yes, but I . . ."

I must have caught something from Quincy, because I cut short a full-grown-up woman. "Would you pay her for doing it?"

Miss Lizzy sighed again. "But, Biddy, I already pay you and Quincy to take care of me. And this is something extra I want Quincy to do."

"Yes, ma'am, but we live here. You asked us to sit

at your table. It's different than Quincy working extra hours at the Brown Cow."

"I don't see that . . ."

I done it again. I was for sure catching a bad case of Quincy-mouth. "When I come to you. Asked you to draw me a map to the feed store. Did I pay you?"

Miss Lizzy was getting some smarter. She didn't talk.

"I asked you a favor, like a friend."

Miss Lizzy looked off out the window.

"I'm sorry if I'm not explaining it right. I can't get things lined up in my head."

Miss Lizzy turned back to me. "I think you explained it the best way anyone could."

I took those words straight upstairs with me. Talked them right on a tape, 'cause I don't never want to forget them.

Quincy

I put in my hours at the Brown Cow. I kept myself to myself most of yesterday and Jen and Ellen purty much give up trying to get me to be friendly, so I fret and chop and clean without no one bothering me. At home I fix dinner and for sure felt like having me a nap. I'm tired to the bone from seein' Robert 'round every corner when he ain't really there, I'm weary of jumpin' at every noise and thinkin' badness is right there coming to get me, and I'm just sad when I look down at my stomach.

But Lizabeth's important friend was coming. Lizabeth had a cheesecake from the bakery, so I guess she thought I'd poison her dead if I made the dessert. I was too tired to get stirred up about it.

Me and Biddy took showers and got on our good dresses and tromped to Lizabeth's. I commenced to slice up the cheesecake and make a tray. I got out white napkins, made tea, and went into the dining room to fetch the silver tea set. I heard voices in the living room and look in.

I almost drop the tea tray. I knew the woman setting on the couch.

It was the judge's wife. What could Lizabeth be thinking? She couldn't let Biddy meet this woman.

Biddy

Quincy come in from the dining room toting the silver tea set. She hardly got the tray to the table in one piece, she was shaking so hard.

"Biddy, you got to listen to me. . . ."

"Biddy," Miss Lizzy called from the living room. "Could you come in here, please?"

Quincy grabbed hold of my arm. "Don't go. I'll tell you why later. Don't go in there."

"Quincy, what you so scaredy of? Who's in there?"

"It's the judge's wife, and I'll tell you why you don't want to meet her back at our 'partment, but . . ."

I patted Quincy's hand just like Miss Lizzy does me. "Don't worry your head, Quincy. I know 'bout the Mrs. Judge."

"No," Quincy said. "You don't."

"You know what my granny said to me after I had my baby?"

Quincy stared at me.

"She said, 'The rich gets richer and the poor gets children and sometimes the rich gets the poor's children.'"

"But . . ."

I hushed Quincy. "Granny said that when we was in the store. Mrs. Judge was pushing a pretty little blue-eyed baby in a stroller."

Quincy let go my arm. "I still don't think you should oughta go in there. That woman ain't here to make some poor girl's dream come true."

I smiled at Quincy. "You don't know my dream."

Quincy

I grab holt of Biddy's hand. "I ain't letting you go in there alone."

Biddy squeeze my hand and smile. It didn't light her face none at all. She was scared no matter how brave she talk.

We walk through the dining room and into the living room. Lizabeth and the judge's wife set in big chairs and they talk in low voices that didn't sound friendly. Lizabeth look mad around her mouth and scared in her eyes and sad in the way she set in the chair.

She look away from her important visitor and hitch up her spine.

"Biddy, please, sit down. Quincy, I would consider it a favor if you would fix the tea."

Biddy sat on the divan and I plunk myself right down next to her. "I ain't leavin' Biddy here by her ownself."

Lizabeth all but roll her eyes. "Quincy, we're not going to boil the girl in a pot."

"Let her stay, Elizabeth. I don't want tea." The judge's wife look at Biddy and I could see her bottom lip kinda straighten out, like she caught a whiff of cauliflower.

"Biddy, I'm sure you are a very nice girl. But Elizabeth is confused about a few things and I want to set them straight."

That woman's mouth might say "nice," but her voice didn't.

"Janice, stop right now." Lizabeth stood up.

"You wanted us to talk, so I'm talking," the woman said.

Lizabeth looked frantic. "Biddy, I know I asked you to come in here, but I'm asking you to leave now. I need to speak to my friend alone for a moment."

"No, you don't, Elizabeth. You opened this can of worms. Now I'm closing it," the judge's wife say.

Lizabeth look all scared in her face. "Biddy, I'm asking you again to leave. Janice, this girl knows nothing about anything. I just wanted you to meet her."

"Ridiculous. You're making trouble, Elizabeth." The judge's wife turned and faced Biddy.

"Elizabeth seems to think that since you had a child at about the same time my husband and I adopted one that . . ." She stop talking. And flick a look at Lizabeth that could have set grass on fire. "Elizabeth thinks that I adopted your baby."

Biddy didn't say nothing.

"Well, that's not the case." I saw the judge's wife's bottom lip get a wiggle in it, and I knew for sure she was lying. I also knew for sure that she was covering up scared with mean.

Biddy say, "I know."

"You know?" I jerk Biddy's hand. "What kind of fool talk is that? That baby is yours and I know it."

"Dear girl, you don't know a thing," the judge's wife say. She try to stare me down, but that woman and me—we knew how each other's insides work.

"Don't tell me what I don't know. I heard my foster folk talk about this five years ago."

"What could your foster parents know about me?" The scared was out there to see now.

"My foster mother was a lawyer woman for the ACLU. She tole her husband about a judge that sign papers that let a retarded girl's grandmother say the girl was . . . I don't know, something about not being smart enough to decide things for her ownself. She say the judge sign the papers because him and his wife wanted to adopt the baby."

The woman look at me like I just slap her 'crosst the face.

"And I ain't your 'dear girl,' neither," I say.

"Janice," Lizabeth say as she sat back down. She put her hands to the sides of her head and rubbed like she was tired. "This is a small town. And this is the worst-kept secret in it. My husband was the mayor. You don't think he knew what a judge was doing? You don't think nurses tell stories? You don't think people that work for Child Protective Services don't know how this adoption was managed? Your child will hear it soon enough."

The judge's wife stand and smooth out her skirt. "No, she won't. Because none of this is true." She look at Biddy and talk slow with her words all apart like Biddy was deaf. "My baby was born in Russia. I flew there to get her. I'm sorry about your child, but I'm sure it has a better home than a girl with your . . . problems could give her. Lily is *not* your child. Do not think that. Do not tell anyone she is. Do not come near my child, my home, or me. Do you understand?"

Biddy nod.

"Biddy," I say, real loud.

"Hush, Quincy," Biddy say. "Everything is OK."

"Janice," Lizabeth say, "I didn't want you two to meet so that Biddy could take your child or bother you." She turned to Biddy. "And, Biddy, I didn't mean to bring up painful memories for you. I didn't think that you knew . . ." Her voice trail off, and she look at the judge's wife again. "I just didn't know what else to do. This whole affair is a disgrace. I guess what I really wanted was to assure you that Biddy is a lovely girl. To encourage you to let her into your life a bit, and yes, maybe to shame you into letting her see her baby. And since the cat is out of the bag, I think the least you can do is to assure her that her child is loved and protected."

Biddy smiled a faraway kinda smile then. "Miss Lizzy, that's just what the Mrs. Judge did." She stand up and let loose my hand. "Good-bye, Mrs. Judge. I know your baby ain't mine." And she walk out. Her back straight as a princess.

The judge's wife drop into her chair. She cover up her eyes with her hands. "Elizabeth, how could you do this? The last thing I wanted was to be cruel to that girl."

Lizabeth teared up too. "I never meant that to happen. I'm a meddling old fool." She wiped her eyes with her hanky. "I thought if you met her and knew she would never want to take Lily . . . that you might bring the child here and allow Biddy to see her maybe just once. Just one time." Lizabeth's eyes seemed to go far away when she say that, and her voice got all tight. "Maybe someday you'd feel safe enough to tell her that the child was hers."

I left them talking and went to Biddy. She was cutting cake.

"I'm thinking about going in there and setting that woman's hair on fire," I say.

"Quincy, the Mrs. Judge was just being a good Mama Duck."

Biddy

Mrs. Judge thought I wanted my baby back. Who knows? If I was smart enough to know how, maybe I might of tried. All I know is that baby belongs to her now. She'll never leave her. That makes me feel real good. But I still wish I could ever have held her. Sung her a song.

I wish Miss Lizzy hadn't never made us meet. The way it was, I could make believe that my baby's mother might like me. It's like if you get one thing, you gotta lose something else. I know my baby's new mama loves her. But it hurts me down deep to know Mrs. Judge thinks I'm trash.

Her name is Lily.

Quincy

I slap the tea tray down without saying boo or squat and left them women to fend for they ownselfs. I went to see after Biddy.

I found her in her room, digging in a little box like a squirrel looking for nuts.

"What you up to?"

Biddy turnt 'round and she helt a handful of tapes. "I'm gonna throw these away."

"Why?"

"I made 'em so my baby could have remembery. But she got her own remembery. Mine will make her feel bad."

I husht because I could see Biddy had her head set. I trail after her to the kitchen. She open the cabinet under the sink and helt the tapes over the trash can. I could see it hard to let her words be garbage. But she jerk her hand open and the tapes slide in.

Biddy went to her room and I wait till she close her door, and I snatch them tapes out the trash. Who knows? That little ole baby gonna know she didn't come from Russia when she can't talk no Russia talk. And she might want to know where she did come from. Shoot-a-goose, you never know what could happen tomorrow—much less a long time from tomorrow.

I needed to take me another long hot shower. It had been a bad day, and bad days made thoughts of Robert crowd in on me.

Quincy

Biddy done quit making her tapes. Said she don't have no reason to make 'em. I don't talk on my tape every night like I used to, just sometimes. Biddy walk to the Brown Cow and back with me every day and we talk. We talk about Lizabeth apologizin' to Biddy for "ambushin'" her. Biddy tell Lizabeth that she know she just doin' what she thought best. I stayed some mad at Lizabeth for a while but easied down when I saw that Biddy was OK.

But what Lizabeth did was bad wrong. Maybe she meant to do a good thing, but she's a full-grown woman and she ain't no Speddie and should know when right is right and wrong is wrong. How can I trust her anymore? It's hard knowing that real people can make mistakes just like girls like us.

Quincy

But they's one thing I hasn't talk to Biddy about.

I seen Robert yesterday.

I was on my break at the Brown Cow. It was looking like rain and I wanted to smell that fresh, good rain smell. And Robert was sitting there in the parking lot. He was in his friend's car. I start back to the big doors, afraid he was gonna jump out that car and grab me. But his friend start up the motor. He pull out to go into the street, and Robert lean his whole shoulders and chest out the window and yell, "I know where you live, Ho. I know your stupid friend live there too. I know about that rich old lady."

He put his finger up and made like he cut his throat with a knife. Then he howl like a wild animal.

Quincy

I don't know what to do. If I tell Biddy, she be scared as me. Lizabeth might fall over dead if she know some evil-minded boy know where she live and that she rich.

Maybe I should just run away. That way Biddy and Lizabeth be safe, and Robert couldn't find me neither. But I don't know no place to run to.

Ms. Delamino can't help me. Nobody wants to live with me now. Who would want to live with me with some evil boy after her and anybody 'round her?

If I tell Lizabeth what that boy done to me, would she think I was trash?

The police ain't gonna believe no kinda girl like me if I tole anything. Folks like me ain't worth they trouble.

I dreamed me some fierce, evil dreams when I finally slept.

Quincy

This morning after my hot shower with plenty of hard scrubbin', I packed me up a bag. I was for sure that I was goin' to be leavin' this little 'partment soon. I went next door and I made oatmeal and sliced peaches and buttered-up toast. Lizabeth came in and we ate, but only Biddy and her was doing the talking. When Biddy stood up to take the plates, I said, "I be needing to tell you something."

Lizabeth made a frown. "I sensed that something was troubling you, Quincy."

"My trouble 'bout to spill onto both of you now."

Biddy's eyes got all round, and she sat back down. She shook her head like to tell me not to say nothing.

"Biddy, I got to do this. I been thinking hard."

I tole Lizabeth about what Robert done. That ole lady turn almost gray in the face, but she kept her shoulders straight and her eyes locked onto mine. I tole it all.

I 'spected Lizabeth to tell me to get right on out her house, but then she said something that made the world turn backwards and do the sidestroke. She didn't say nothing 'bout me bringing this on my ownself. She didn't say that I had to get out her house. She didn't say that I was stupid and now some crazy mean boy might break in her house and knock her on her head.

"Oh, Quincy. What can I do to help you?" she said. She had tears in her eyes, but they didn't tumble down her cheek. Just looking at that ole woman make me feel . . . strong, maybe. I didn't feel dirty.

Biddy and me, we look at each other like monkeys done jumped out that ole lady's mouth and danced on they hands.

"I can help you with the police if you decide to report this . . ." She pinch her lips together. "Well, I won't say out loud what I think he is."

"NO!" Biddy jump out her chair so hard she knock it backwards. "No, Quincy cain't tell nobody else."

Lizabeth got all soft-eyed. "Oh, Biddy, I think I can understand why you would say that. I can see that Quincy is afraid too." She shook her head. Then she put her hand on my hand. "Quincy, you are a woman. You can make your own decisions—I'm not going to meddle and risk making things worse. I can't force you to tell the police. But I think you should."

"I tole you about all this," I said to Lizabeth, "not 'cause I want you to help with the police. But 'cause I feel wrong, letting Robert be out there, watching you and Biddy, without you knowing that he could hurt you."

Biddy got her chair back up and sat. She lean across the table like getting close made what she said easier to understand.

"You ain't by yourself no more. You got us to watch for you. And I can watch for that old Robert."

Biddy, she was talking brave, but I could see the scared in her face.

"Do you think this Robert will harm us?" Lizabeth axt.

"Not if I don't open my mouth. I don't think he want nothing but to make sure I don't get him in trouble. I think if we don't say nothin', then we's safe."

"But what about the harm that he's done to you already? Doesn't that count?"

Biddy and I both look down at the table. I could hardly make my voice come out my throat. "Lizabeth, peoples like you count. People like me, it just different."

"One day, I hope, you'll know that you're wrong about that," Lizabeth say.

Next thing I knowed all three of us was having us a snot-nosed crying jag.

Quincy

I thought about it a long time. I thought whilst I work on Biddy's present. I thought whilst I chop and dice at the Brown Cow. I thought whilst Biddy watch the TV. I got tired thinking so hard. I felt like giving up, and sometimes I just cried and Biddy had to make me coffee to bring me around.

"Biddy," I said, "what if we wrong? What if them police ain't like your granny? I got these scars on me. Them police won't think I done that to myself."

Biddy sigh and she turnt off the TV. "We orphans, and the policemans they know that. They don't care what happen. They don't care if you tell the truth or not."

I tug at my hair like it could make my head bigger and some smart could get inside. "We ain't orphans. We got a mother and father somewhere. They ain't dead."

"Quincy, we're . . . heart orphans. Never had nobody that loved us. That makes us different. It ain't because you a mix-up race. It ain't because I had a child that got took away. Why should policemans care what happen if nobody ever cared?"

I didn't say nothing. I laid down on my bed.

Quincy

I never been close to nobody. I always knew not to love nobody 'cause I'd just get taken away and put in another home. People were mean to me more than they was ever nice. The ones that were nice were ones that was paid. Like Ms. Evans and Ms. D., and, well, even Mr. Hallis and the other foster folks got paid.

But there was a feeling I had when Biddy tole me stuff and Lizabeth pet my hand. A feelin' that pulled me close.

Quincy

Biddy be wrong. I care that Robert might hurt her 'cause of me. Lizabeth tried to make it so Biddy could see her took-away baby. If Biddy got two peoples that care about her and what happen to her, then she ain't no heart orphan no more. Is she?

Quincy

Biddy, she come out in the world, even in the dark when I was late from work. That fool girl was worried 'bout me. She still walkin' me to and from the Brown Cow. Lizabeth didn't put me out her house or even this 'partment. She even had a taxicab come fetch us and took me to a doctor lady that did tests on my blood and checked me out to see if Robert done me any kind of bad that I wasn't smart enough to wonder 'bout yet. Nobody paid Biddy and Lizabeth to do none of that. That means I ain't no heart orphan anymore neither, don't it?

Quincy

But it might not be any different. Lizabeth, she old and she could up and croak anytime. Biddy, she getting purtier and braver ever day. Some boy might come along and want to be her boyfriend. I'd be an orphan again.

All this thinking making me crazy-headed.

Quincy

I gathered Lizabeth and Biddy 'round some presents all wrapped up nice in the middle of the table.

"Is it someone's birthday?" Lizabeth axt.

"Nope, this is a 'just because Quincy say so' day," I say.

Biddy and Lizabeth set down and look at me.

"I have presents for everybody." I hand the first one to Biddy. "Open it."

She grin big and take off the ribbon and the paper real slow, making sure not to ruin the littlest piece. It took her a long time, but I didn't holler at her to hurry up. Sometimes taking extra care is a fine way.

"It's a book," Biddy said. "I can't read no book."

"You can read this one," I say.

Biddy open it. "It's a cookbook."

I made Biddy a cookbook of all the recipes that Mr. Hallis made me. Only instead of words like "cup" and "teaspoon" and "lettuce" and "chicken," there was drawings. It had took me forever.

Biddy got tears in her eyes. "A book I can read." She hug it 'gainst her chest and didn't say nothing else. I felt some good.

I hand another present to Biddy. "This for you too."

She open it. "It's a tape."

Lizabeth look at it. "It's nursery songs."

"I called Ms. D.," I said. "If you want to do it, Ms. D. can set you up to help in the hospital nursery. You got to take a class and wear a uniform, but then you can hold babies for one hour a week. You can sing to 'em if you want."

Nobody said nothing. But this time the nothing was chuck full of sumpin'.

"If you don't want to hold no babies, it's OK, but if you do . . . well, you got to learn sumpin' more than 'Itsy-Bitsy Spider.'"

Before they could say anything, I hand a package to Lizabeth.

Now, Lizabeth, she be my kind of woman. She tore into that package with ribbon and paper flying in the air.

"A camera."

"Somebody in every fambly got to be the picture taker. A fambly takes pictures at Christmas and birthdays and suchlike, don't they?"

Lizabeth look at that camera, then put her hand up in front her eyes.

"And I need you to promise me something," I say.

Lizabeth clear her throat and wipe her eyes.

"I know you old and might"—I tried to think of a polite way to say it—"be pushing up daisies sooner than later. But try not to die on us too soon. OK?"

Quincy

Lizabeth, she made the phone call like I axt her. The policeman say he would come in a car and pick me up so I could make a statement.

Lizabeth and Biddy, they got right in that police car and hold my hand all the way. They sat by me and hold my hand while that policeman make a tape of what I said about Robert. They wouldn't leave even when the police lady took pictures of my scars.

Biddy tole that policeman how she find me in the alley. How she washed my clothes.

Lizabeth said that we had done what we thought was right, but that there was no every-dence but my good word.

That policeman look at me and he say, "Ms. Ford."

Biddy say, "Who Ms. Ford?"

I got to say, it took me a bit of a time to figure it out too. "Biddy, that's me." I don't guess Biddy ever heard my whole name. I cain't remember me a time when anybody used it. Everybody call me Quincy. Even if they don't know me none.

I straighten up my back. And I look at that policeman. All of a sudden, I knew Lizabeth had been right. Maybe folks like Biddy and me not different. He done call me Ms. Ford.

"Ms. Ford, Robert and his buddy are well known at this station. They're both bad actors."

I frowned 'cause I didn't understand what that meant. And I knew he'd think I was stupid.

But that policeman say, "I'm sorry. That was sort of station-house slang. I meant that Robert and his friend act badly." He clear his throat. "Those scars on your stomach are evidence—enough that we can get Robert and Darrel into the station." He tell me them boys was cowards, and maybe he could have them pointing they fingers one at the other. "We'll do our best to bring them to justice for what they have done." He tole me that what I done was the best thing to keep Lizabeth and Biddy and me safe. And he tole me that I was keeping Robert from hurting some other girl later on.

I walk out that station house with my fambly hanging on to my hands.

I knew that Biddy and me—both of us—we wasn't nobody. We count.

Quincy

Sometime I hear a loud car and I think Robert is out there waiting to hurt me. Sometime I get mad at Biddy and Lizabeth. Sometime I get mad at my ownself. I still think this world be harder for folks like me and Biddy than for folks that are smart and don't have a smash-up face.

But sometime Biddy be singing 'bout somebody comin' 'round a mountain and she cleaning like a fool, but she happy. Sometime I cook something extra good and we all smile at one another. Sometime we get laughin' fits. Sometime I don't worry. Sometime I do. Sometime I want to box Lizabeth's ears. Sometime I think I gonna buy Biddy a pet. Something that won't try to eat Mama Duck if she come back. Sometime I think I need to stuff that girl's cleaning rags in my ears so's I cain't hear her singing.

Every once in a while, I hug that fool girl.

Just for nothing.

ACKNOWLEDGMENTS

First, foremost, and well, just always: thanks to Scott Treimel, my trusty agent—and I mean "trusty" in all the best definitions of the word. He believed in this book from the beginning and never, ever let it go. Thanks, my friend.

And to Pam Whitlock, who would never quit bugging me to get this one into print: here it is.

Thank you to the SCBWI and the Judy Blume Grant for helping this book along the road.

And many thanks to my wonderful editor. What graceful direction Andrea Tompa used to get me to make this book what it is.